IF YOU READ THIS

KEREEN GETTEN

Pushkin Children's

Pushkin Press
65–69 Shelton Street
London WC2H 9HE

If You Read This was first published by Pushkin Press in 2022

1 3 5 7 9 8 6 4 2

ISBN 13: 978-1-78269-281-2

Designed and typeset by Tetragon, London
Printed and bound by Clays Ltd, Elcograf S.p.A.

www.pushkinpress.com

IF YOU
READ THIS

KEREEN GETTEN grew up in Jamaica where she would climb fruit trees in the family garden and eat as much mango, guinep and pear as she could without being caught. She now lives in Birmingham with her family and writes stories about her childhood experiences. Her debut novel *When Life Gives You Mangoes*, also published by Pushkin Children's, was shortlisted for the Waterstones Children's Book Prize, the Spark Award, Warwickshire Junior Book Award and the Jhalak Children's & YA Prize.

IF YOU READ THIS

I

The night before my birthday, Mama would always slip a note under my door. It would read:

Dear Ms Brie,
   Thank you for staying at the Wonderland Hotel. We want to give you the experience of a lifetime, so to begin, please check your choices for breakfast in the morning:
   CEREAL
   PORRIDGE
   FRUIT: MANGO
   FRUIT: BANANA

FRUIT: PINEAPPLE

FRUIT: ALL THREE

EGG: SCRAMBLED

EGG: FRIED

EGG: OMELETTE

EGG: ALL THREE

BACON

SAUSAGE

PLANTAIN

ACKEE & SALTFISH

TEA

HOT CHOCOLATE

MILO

ORANGE JUICE

WATER

After Mama died, and after I could think about her again without crying, I would slip Mama's menu under Nana's door the night before my birthday, just like Mama used to slip the menu under mine. Every year, I listen for her to go to bed, and giggle under my pillow when she finds it. "What is this? This girl really takes me for a hotel." But every morning for the last three years, I've woken to the smell of breakfast, and all the foods on my list.

That was Nana. Always making a fuss when I asked her for something but doing it anyway.

This morning, though, I don't smell the food I asked for. So I jump out of bed to see if Nana got my note last night.

The frilly dress she buys every year hangs on the back of the door. I ignore it and throw on one of my nicer tops and a pair of black shorts instead.

When I come out of my room, I hear voices and the faint sound of music. I enter the living room from the hallway and peer to the left into the small kitchen at the back of the house. The walls are bright green, painted over from when Mama woke one day and painted the entire kitchen pink because she saw it in a dream. She and Papa argued that day. He said no one painted their kitchen pink, and it made his head hurt.

Mama said, "Then we will be the first, and your head will get used to it."

From the living room, I can see Nana bustling around with her back to me. She's wearing a long pink dress that is supposed to match my frilly one.

Hers makes her look like an overgrown doll, but for some reason Nana likes to find us matching clothes for special occasions.

"Nana?" I call, entering the kitchen. I look around, confused. There is no food. The table is empty. Maybe she's finally had enough of my requests.

She spins around, surprised. "What are you doing up?" she cries, then peers out the window before returning her gaze to me. Her long white hair sits on her shoulders, styled in the big curls she always wears when she dresses up. Nana has had the same hairstyle since I was born, and before, because I've seen photos of her back in the 1800s and her hair was the same then too. She's tried to put make-up on over her usually bare skin, but Nana isn't very good at make-up and her eyeliner makes her look like a pirate.

I frown. "It's what people do in the morning, Nana. They wake up."

She looks around, distracted. "Yes... yes, they do, but you think you can go back?"

I stare at her. "Go back?"

She nods, glancing out the window. "Yes, maybe go and change into that dress I left out for you."

I point down to what I'm wearing. "Nana, I can't do the six-year-old Sunday-school look any more."

She looks at me, exasperated. "You can't make your Nana happy this one time, Brie? I'm an old woman and I only have one wish."

I let out a loud groan, throwing my face to the ceiling. "Nooooo, not the last-wish blackmail."

She fidgets with the tray in her hand. "It's just a dress."

"It's an embarrassment to dresses. All the other dresses disowned it. Even the shop owner didn't want it in the shop no more." I continue to moan about the dress, but she has already turned away.

"Put the dress on, Brie."

"The lady who made it threw it away because she regretted making it."

"Bridgette..."

"I bet there's a petition on social media demanding that this dress never be seen by human eyes."

"All I ask from you is one thing..."

"I'll die. The dress will kill me. I... can't... breathe..." I pretend to collapse.

Aunty Elsa, Papa's sister, appears in the doorway, eyes beaming. "Brie," she says, surprised, then turns to Nana and whispers, "We're ready."

Nana heads towards the back door. She looks over her shoulder at me. "Brie, put on the dress. I'm not going to ask you again."

I drag my feet back to my room and stare at the frilly pink dress hanging on the back of the door. I sigh and take it off the hanger. At least it's only my family seeing me in this dress. It could be worse—the whole town could see me wearing it.

*

"Happy Birthday!" a chorus of voices shouts in unison.

I step outside to lots of familiar faces looking back at me. Everyone is here. My two best friends—Smiley and Femi—and their parents; Dion, my neighbour; and Dion's three younger brothers, all wearing the same white shirt, bow tie and blue jeans because their parents couldn't be bothered to buy them different clothes. Aunty Elsa, Papa's sister and her boyfriend, Julius. There are more neighbours and people from school who I barely speak to but Nana thinks are my friends because they're on my football team.

Our back garden has been transformed with fairy lights and balloons in the trees. A long table covered with a pink and white cloth is filled with food, drinks and a three-tier cake covered in pink icing. White chairs line the long table, and a separate, smaller table to the left is piled high with presents. But all I can see are people. People now staring back at me in my pink frilly dress. I feel sick.

Great. As if my life couldn't get any worse. I edge backward towards the house, but Nana reaches for my arm and links hers with mine.

"Nuh-uh. Don't you dare," she says through clenched teeth, forcing me to stay until they finish singing.

"Speech!" Julius shouts, and Aunty Elsa elbows him.

I close my eyes, hoping that when I open them this will all have been a dream. I hate attention. I can see the expectations as they wait for me to say something nice when all I want to do is run.

I clear my throat, wishing I could clear my back-yard of all these people, but no. They're still here.

"Nana made me wear it," I say, pointing to the dress and the shoes.

An awkward silence falls among them except for a snort from Uncle Julius.

Nana turns to the sea of bemused faces. "Everyone, take a seat before the food gets cold," she announces.

They all sit down at the long table, while I am still rooted to the step.

Nana shoots me a look. "What's wrong with you?"

I want to tell her that if she hadn't forced me to wear the dress, none of this would have happened. Better still, if she hadn't invited the entire neighbourhood, she wouldn't feel so humiliated right now.

"Go and sit down and act like you want to be here," she says, before painting on a smile and asking everyone if they need anything.

I find a spot between Smiley and Femi and sit down, grateful that at least the table hides most of the outfit.

The table is buzzing with chatter as the sun rises higher behind us. Jackfruit, the local tourist guide, is playing music from five hundred years ago, and Nana is hobbling around the table with her bad hip, asking everyone if they need anything.

"Cool speech, Brie," Dion says from across the table.

My face gets hot, and I nearly choke on my pineapple. It's not that Dion and I have never talked—we used to talk all the time. Mama would take him to nursery with me when we were small, but then we got older, and he became cool and popular and I didn't. He got new friends and we grew apart.

We're so different now. I cringe when I think about the days I used to make him dress up as a doll and play make-believe.

Smiley nudges me under the table. "Don't ignore him," she hisses behind her hand. "Say something back."

I purse my lips at her before switching to a smile when I realize Dion is looking.

"Thank you for not coming," I blurt out.

Smiley and Femi snort with laughter on either side of me.

*

As the table empties, Aunty Elsa approaches me from behind. "You ready for your presents?"

This is my favourite part of my birthday. Not because I expect big, expensive things—we don't have enough money for that. This is when I get to see if Nana and Papa have picked up on any of my hints in the past six months. It also means I don't have to stand in front of everyone again in this dress.

What I really want is a better phone so I won't get laughed at any more at school or want to hide it in my pocket when someone calls me. I only got a phone three years ago because Nana wanted a way to contact me if she was going to be late picking me up from school.

I wrap my arms around myself and follow her over to a smaller table. "Where's Papa?" I ask, suddenly realizing he is not in the crowd.

"He had to rush into work," Aunty Elsa tells me, "but he'll be back soon."

My heart sinks, and I try to hide how disappointed I am that he can't even be here for my birthday. I should be used to this by now. This isn't new; this is all the time. If it isn't my birthday, it's the school play or sports day. Papa is rarely around: work is always more important than me.

I feel Aunty Elsa's arm around my shoulder.

"He'll be here," she whispers in my ear.

I force a smile and push down the knot in my throat. Swallowing it hurts every time as though it's the first time. I'm embarrassed and hurt that Papa can't take a few hours off for my birthday. Aunty Elsa and Julius could do it; even our neighbours could be here. But not Papa. It's as if spending time with me is the hardest thing for him.

I take a deep breath and bite my lip as Nana joins us at the table. She and Aunty Elsa surround me, kissing my face and stroking my hair, neither of them saying a word, but I know what they're telling me—that it's OK.

Nana picks up a small box covered with silver wrapping paper and hands it to me. "Right, this one first," she says. She beams at me the way Nana does when she wants me to do the same, to smile.

So I do what she asks: I force a smile that hides my disappointment.

"It's from your father," Nana says, "to store things in. He bought it from the wood carver on the beach."

I stare inside the box and wonder when he found the time to get this when he barely has time for me. Maybe, just like for Christmas and other people's birthdays, he gives Nana a list so she can buy my presents for him.

"It's nice," I murmur.

"Pick ours next," Julius calls from the table. Aunty Elsa glares at him. "What?" he says, throwing his hands in the air. "She just opened an empty box. Ours will look like gold." He chuckles to himself but stops abruptly when Nana shoots him a look.

Nana hands me presents one by one, and the morning moves slowly, like when you're in your last class at school and the clock doesn't seem to move.

Nana has a story for every present, or she forces whoever bought the present to stand up and tell everyone why they chose that present, and I wish she wouldn't talk so long. I wish she wouldn't make such a big deal over every present. I don't understand why everyone is here. Half these people weren't here for my eleventh birthday or my tenth, so why are they here now? Why this birthday? What's the big deal about being twelve?

Her voice swims in and out like a wave and I try to focus. I try to smile, and I try to remember to say thank you for every present I open. But my heart isn't in it because Papa isn't here.

I get a hamper basket from Smiley and Femi, filled with all my favourite chocolates and a bag of tamarind balls. A locket with a photo of the family, including Mama, from Uncle Julius and Aunty Elsa. The photo is old. I look about three years old in it and Papa is smiling so I know it's old. I stare at the photo, remembering how things changed so much after Mama died. How one day everything was perfect and then it wasn't.

"Thank you, Aunty Elsa and Uncle Julius."

Dion's mother gets me perfume. Nana gets me a pair of white trainers.

"The lady at the shop told me all the kids are wearing them," she says, nodding to the box in my hand.

I see movement from the corner of my eye and look up expecting to see Papa, but it's not; it's Uncle Julius getting more food. I return my empty gaze to the shoebox.

"Thanks, Nana," I mumble without looking up.

I'm hoping this is it and Nana will send everyone home so I can stop pretending.

"There's one more," Nana says, and my heart sinks. She looks over to the house, frowning. "Where's your father? He's supposed to be here for this."

"I'll call him," Julius says, taking out his phone and walking away from the table.

We wait in silence as he calls Papa's phone, Nana with the final gift box in her hand and Aunty Elsa with her arms tightly around my shoulder. We wait in silence, except for Dion's three brothers, who start hitting each other.

Julius turns and shakes his head, slipping the phone back in his pocket. "Some emergency at work," he says, giving me a quick, reassuring smile. "He says to carry on but he will be here as soon as he can."

The embarrassment of what people must be thinking weighs heavy. I can imagine what they are saying under their breaths. *Why isn't he here? It's her birthday.* I avoid their eyes so I can't see what they are thinking. I twist my fingers to stop myself from feeling.

Nana sighs, exchanging a look with Aunty Elsa before her eyes lower to the box in her hand. I feel Aunty Elsa's fingers pressing into my skin. I feel her body stiffen beside me and I look at her. She forces a smile, stroking my shoulder, but her eyes are misty, as though she is about to cry. I'm confused about why Aunty Elsa is so upset that Papa's not here.

Nana looks down at the box, but instead of handing it to me, she holds it close to her chest. She pauses, then looks over at Aunty Elsa next to me. "If her father isn't here to do it, then it should be you."

Aunty Elsa lets go of me and moves over to Nana and takes the box. They both glance at me with a look I have seen so many times, the one that says *Poor girl, poor Brie*. I feel a knot in my stomach, and I press my hands into the fold of my dress.

"This," Aunty Elsa says, looking down at the box. "This is from your mama."

And it's as if I lose my breath.

2

I remember Mama like the waves on the seashore. She comes in and out of my mind when something I do, see or hear reminds me of her. Like when a song comes on the radio reminding me of how much she loved to sing. Mama would sing to every song even when she didn't know the words.

My mother was like fire. She lit up the room in all her colours. She wasn't anything like Papa. She was the opposite of him. She changed her hair every week and had a hundred wigs for every occasion. Blue for Saturdays, short for Sundays, red and long for Mondays, curly for Wednesdays.

She was loud, the kind of loud you could hear on the other side of the room. The kind of loud that made me cringe with embarrassment.

Her laughter was like your favourite song that you put on repeat. You wanted—no, needed—to hear it over and over again. I used to hate Mama's laugh; people always stared because she was so loud. I just didn't know it back then, how much I needed to hear it. How safe I found her voice.

My mother would wake me in the morning and whisper, "Get dressed. We're going on an adventure," without telling Papa we were leaving. She would hand me one of her long dresses that were always too big for me, making it fit with a belt, and one of her oversized hats. We would take the early bus to the nearest town while people stared at what we were wearing, but she did not care. She would sing loudly to the song on the radio even when I told her people were looking. She would laugh and wave at them, then tell me to join her.

She was the kind of mother who stuck her head out the window to inhale the wind. She was the kind of mother who gently lifted my head with her finger every time my eyes dropped to the floor. She was the kind of mother who would take me out of school without telling anyone and have Papa frantically searching for us because he thought something had happened. She was impulsive and wild, and always thought she knew best. Even when I told her I didn't want to miss my favourite class, she would tell me, "You have for ever to learn from books, Brie, but no one else will teach you about living."

Even as the cancer made her sick, she would plan days out in the forest to find waterfalls and have picnics by the river. There were days when she could barely walk and we would be in the middle of nowhere with nothing but birch trees towering above us and bushes surrounding us, and she had to stop every five minutes to rest, but she still wanted her adventures and refused to go back.

Now, three years on, when I remember her, her smile fades in and out of my memory like a dream after you wake. Her touch used to feel like velvet; now it feels like air.

Now, every time Mama tries to enter my mind, I fill it with things to do and places to go and people to see so my brain does not have a second to remember she is no longer here.

I stare at the box in Aunty Elsa's arms and my heart pounds so fast against my chest I think it might explode. Now I am forced to remember her in front of everyone.

"Well, give her the box, nuh." Nana's impatient voice interrupts my thoughts.

There is nervous laughter around me. Aunty Elsa takes my hands and places them around the box.

"From Ma?" I breathe, speaking for the first time since she delivered the news. It seems like for ever since we said her name out loud.

I feel everyone's eyes on me as I take the box from her. I hold it gingerly as though it's going to explode.

"She used to be better at wrapping," I joke, noticing the messy silver wrapping paper hastily put together. "Not like an MC rapper—she couldn't even sing—but like, you know..." My voice trails off, but it is enough to have everyone else laughing. I hear Nana's stilted laughter in my ear.

They fall silent again as I hold the box awkwardly. My head swims with questions too fast for me to catch them.

I look over at Aunty Elsa. "How?" I say, trying to make my voice as light as possible, trying to fill the silence. What I want to do is take this to my room and close the door. I want to sit alone on the bedroom floor and think about what just happened without everyone watching me.

"She was determined to do something for your twelfth birthday," Aunty Elsa says. "Twelve is a big number. You're growing up, getting older, and Dee wanted to be part of that."

I bite my lip hard. So hard it stings. I feel my eyes blur and a lump catch in my throat. After all this time, it still hurts to hear her name.

I pull at the silver wrapping that sparkles when the sun catches it. My mind swirls with the possibilities that could be inside. All the things I told her I wanted when I was nine, or before. The baby things I liked back then but don't like now and how I will have to pretend to like it because it's from Mama.

I tear at the wrapping, and pieces of silver paper float to the ground.

Nana bends down to pick them up. "She always dropping things and not picking them up."

She tuts at me, and I think she just wants to lighten the mood because the air is thick with feelings and everyone is so quiet. Too quiet. Julius laughs loudly as though Nana has just told the funniest joke. Everyone else is silent, and I hear their silence more than I hear his laughter.

Under the wrapping paper is a small box. A light wooden box with a golden clasp and the word BRIDGETTE carved out. There is a heart drawn on the lid like she used to do in every card she wrote, every note she sent. The curve of the heart is squiggly because she always rushed and got frustrated when it wasn't perfect.

"Oh! Now look, it's ruined," she would say. "Should I start again?" She would sit at the kitchen table, her perfectly shaped eyebrows wrinkled, her long, manicured fingers resting against her chin while she considered whether to waste another card.

But it never mattered how many cards she wrote; her hearts were always the same, squiggly on the end.

I run my fingers along the carving, and I feel strangely numb. Sometimes it feels like just yesterday she was here, drawing hearts in cards, making Papa mad by disappearing with me. Sometimes, like now, it feels like it never happened. Like it happened to someone else, somewhere else, and it was just a movie I watched one time.

I open the box and there is a flutter in my stomach. The kind of flutter filled with nerves and excitement. Inside are three pink and white envelopes piled neatly on top of each other, held together by a string. The top envelope reads *Open Me First*. The writing looks strange, not like hers at all, but maybe she wrote it when she was sick. I saw her write a note in the hospital once, and her writing looked like a six-year-old's.

I take a deep breath and draw out the first envelope, laying the box on the floor. My heart beats fast as I stare at the letter, wondering what Mama has to say. Aware that everyone is waiting, nervous it might say something I don't want anyone else to hear.

I rip it open and pull out the pink and white paper. I unfold it and there it is, her familiar writing bouncing off the page. Unlike the writing on the envelope, this is definitely hers; I recognize it straight away. A smile creeps at the side of my mouth and it feels as though she is here, right next to me. As if for this moment, she has returned.

"Well?" Julius shouts. "What does it say?"

Aunty Elsa tells him to shush and leave me be.

"Jackfruit, where that music at?" she shouts.

Music suddenly fills the air, and I take a deep breath of relief. That's why I love Aunty Elsa. She always knows what to say even when I don't.

She gives me a reassuring squeeze and leads Nana away, and as the chatter slowly returns to normal, I stand where they have left me, by the table, with the opened presents, reading Mama's letter in rushed gulps of air.

My Dearest Brie,

If you read this, it's because you have reached that special age. An important milestone that I wish I was there to see. I can't believe you are turning twelve. I'm wondering how tall you are. If you still look like me, or if you are now suffering looking like your papa.

How is school? Are you still friends with Smiley? What do you like doing? What makes you smile?

These are all the questions I wish I knew the answer to. The things I took for granted before.

As I write this, I am sitting under the coconut tree, where you and I have sat many times, reading, singing and making plans to go into the city to watch a movie or into the hills to see your favourite waterfall.

This seemed the perfect place to write you these letters from my heart. Letters to remind you of the joy you brought into my life. Letters to check in on you, make sure you're doing OK.

I wrote you a few letters to be opened over the next few days. These letters say, I miss you, I love you, and I am always with you.

These letters are so we can have one more adventure together. These letters are for you to make new memories. They are to remind you that I will be by your side, always. That I am the breeze in the trees. I am the sun that shines. I am the morning dew and the moon in the sky. I have been here, and will always be with you, by your side, always.

Tomorrow, the adventure starts.
I hope you're ready!
  Happy twelfth birthday, Brie.
  Always Your
     Mama

I read the letter over and over. The first time I read it too fast, and the second and third time I think I may have missed something. The fourth time, I read it as though I am her so I can imagine her writing it. Imagine what she was feeling or thinking. I wonder when she wrote it and where I was at the time. Was I at school? Was I inside doing my homework? Or had I gone with Nana to the market as I often did back then? Was she sick? Or was she having one of her good days? Or did she write them at the end when there were no more days left?

My heart sings a song I have not heard for a long time. I feel full, as though I have just eaten Nana's Saturday soup with the corn and dumpling and potato and meat. But not so full that I'm tired and just want to sleep. I feel so full that I want to scream it to the world. I want to dance on tables and do cartwheels across the yard. I want to hug Nana and kiss Aunty Elsa, and even if Papa shows up late, I will hug him so tight he will ask me if I'm OK. I never knew how much I needed to hear from Mama until now. I never knew how much I missed her.

I skip over to where Smiley and Femi are helping themselves to Nana's famous grater cake with pink sugar icing. I grab them both by the hand and pull them away, spinning them around in a circle.

"What's happening?" Femi says, narrowing her eyes at me while still allowing me to pull her around.

Smiley stuffs the whole grater cake in her mouth and grabs Femi's hand to make a circle. "Brie's dancing!" she shouts with her mouth full. "Who cares why—just go with it."

Slowly Femi relaxes as I lead them in an old dance routine we made up when we were nine. It's only as we fumble through the moves, laughing as we try to remember them, that I realize this is the dance Mama helped us create. At the time I didn't want her to; it was embarrassing having her watch us from the kitchen door, shouting instructions, reminding us how she nearly made it into a nineties music video once. She was always doing that, always interrupting what me and my friends were doing, or suggesting we do something else, something she wanted to do. My friends were always too polite to say no, but I hated it. I hated that I couldn't be with my friends without her poking her nose in.

Today, though, it seems perfect to be doing the dance moves she created. It seems perfect after the letter. Everything seems perfect now, and I forget I am wearing the frilly pink dress as I grab my leg behind me, kicking it out with my left arm against my head, and I think the only thing missing is Papa.

3

As the sun sets, the celebration moves down to the beach. There is a bonfire pit at the edge of the beach that is lit every Saturday night for tourists.

We live in a gated community called North Shore Villas on the north coast of our island. The villas sit behind a security gate with a security guard called Almond, who has a dog called Prince, who isn't very good at guarding.

The villas are owned by foreigners who rent them out to tourists most of the year. A few houses like ours have people who live in them permanently, who work on the resort like Papa, who is the resort manager.

All the villas have weird, random names like Coral Cove Villa or Oh Boy Villa. Our house is called Driftwood, which isn't too bad, but Smiley's house is called Buena Vista. When we looked it up, we saw that it meant 'good view' in Spanish, which is a lie really, because the front of their house faces the road and the back of their house, like all the workers' houses, faces the bush.

Behind our villas are miles of bushes and rocks that lead into the local town. But the long, quiet road outside our villa takes you downhill towards the sea, where a sprawling one-storey building sits with the resort's restaurant, gym and Papa's office.

It's the beginning of summer, and the tourists have been trickling in over the last few days. In a month or so, it will be packed with people from all over the world and we won't be allowed to use the fire pit any more.

Sheila, the cook at the restaurant, brings out a tub of marshmallows so we can do what the Americans like doing and hold them over the fire until they burn. Nana lets me have two because it's my birthday.

She tuts, "Them things too sweet for children."

"Tween, Nana," I correct her, even though all I can think about is Mama's letter.

She frowns at me, then at a grinning Aunty Elsa. "Twee... what?" she says.

Aunty Elsa explains that it means 'almost a teenager', and Nana sucks her teeth, saying she doesn't know where I get these foreign ideas from.

Smiley appears beside me with her marshmallow, and the yellow flame from the fire lights up her face. "So, are you going to tell us?"

"Tell you what?" I ask, pretending not to know what she's talking about. She rolls her eyes. "The letter from your mother?"

Femi joins us with a plate of pineapple slices. "So, what did it say?" she asks.

We sit down on a towel Nana had provided and feel it sink into the warm sand.

Smiley nudges me. "Well, what did it say?"

I feel that flutter again as though I'm about to tell them I won a prize. It's funny how when she was here all she did was embarrass me, but now all I want to do is talk about her and the letter she wrote to me. All day I've been wondering when she wrote the letters. There are so many questions I want to ask Nana when we get home. I glance over at Nana, who is busy in conversation with Aunty Elsa. I wonder if she knew all along. Did she keep this secret for three years? I feel a sudden urge to run over there and hug her, knowing she kept this secret when Nana is so bad at keeping anyone's secret, which is why no one tells her anything.

"So?" Smiley prods me. "What did the letter say? Anything exciting?"

"Did she say she hopes you've turned out to be everything she ever wanted?" Femi says.

So, I tell them about the letter because I can't keep it to myself any more.

"She said she's taking me on an adventure," I tell them, eyes wide with excitement, hoping they feel as excited as I do, and a little jealous.

Femi frowns between bites of her food. "What kind of adventure?"

"Because adults' idea of an adventure is never the same as ours," Smiley agrees.

I roll my eyes, a little frustrated that they're raining on my parade. "No, it's a real adventure, going somewhere special."

Now I have their attention.

"Like where?" Femi asks.

I hesitate, realizing I don't actually know what

the adventure is, and they could be right—Mama's idea of an adventure might be something cringey like picking naseberries and taking them to the neighbours. That excitement I felt before starts to fade as I realize Mama knew me when I was nine. That's the last memory she had of me, so maybe... I have a sinking feeling. Maybe this adventure she planned for me is the same kind of adventure I found exciting when I was nine.

"She didn't say," I admit, deflated. "I have to read the next letter." We fall silent, and the marshmallow suddenly tastes sour and not sweet like it did a few minutes ago.

"Maybe she's sending you overseas or something," Smiley suggests.

Femi looks at her, baffled. "Why would she do that?"

Smiley shrugs. "I dunno. Going overseas is an adventure. Maybe she wants her to travel the world."

They fall silent and I can tell what they're thinking. The same thing I'm thinking—that maybe Mama's adventure isn't going to be an adventure after all.

*

The day after my birthday, I wake thinking about Mama's letters. There is no one around to distract me. No presents to open, no friends to talk to. Only me and the box of letters sitting on my desk across the room.

The smell of fried plantain wafts under the door, and I can hear Nana's favourite radio station playing the news. I lie on my back, staring at the ceiling. I don't know why Nana likes listening to the news every day, only to complain how depressing the news is.

"What?" I hear her shout over the radio. "Again? Lord have mercy."

My head hurts. Like when you're sick and it feels like someone is pressing on your brain. I check my temperature in case I am sick, but I don't know what I'm looking for. How hot is too hot? I roll over onto my side, staring at the box across the room. The excitement from seeing the letters for the first time yesterday has faded, and now all I feel is nervous.

Mama used to say that I overthink too much. That I make things worse than they are just by making up stories in my head. "Stop overthinking so much," she would say. "All it does is make everything worse."

I take a deep breath and swing my feet off the bed and onto the floor, but I'm interrupted by Nana yelling my name.

"Brie! Get up. Breakfast ready."

I glance at the box, then at the door. Nana will call me a few more times before she comes looking for me, and all I want is to read the next letter, to see what adventures Mama has for me.

I walk over to my desk, which is cluttered with schoolwork and books that I should be reading over the holidays. I pick up the box and carry it over to my bed, sitting down on the edge with a sigh.

I open the box and take out the next letter, and just like last night, my heart skips a beat seeing her writing across the page.

My Dearest Brie,

If you read this, then it is because you have read the first letter and you want to know more, and that fills me with joy.

When I think about you, I think about our adventures around town. The games that we played, the

treasure hunts that kept you enter-
tained for hours.

So, this is another treasure hunt.
One that I hope will keep you enter-
tained for years to come.

I want to give you something special that I have held on to for years as
my own. A secret few people know. It
was something I was hoping to share
with you myself, at the right time.
My dream was to be there, to see your
face, to hear your reaction. What joy
we would have had together on this
adventure. But instead, I will sit here
in my bed, where I seem to be every
day these days! And I will imagine
it as though it is happening right
now, in front of me.

So, here is your clue:

To find the secret, your father
must take you to the place where
summer never ends. To the place
filled with adventure. The island of
fairy tales.

When you get there, open the next letter for more instructions.
Always Your
Mama x

I feel my heart pounding against my chest as I reread the letter, a smile pulling at my lips as I think about this adventure Mama has planned for me. I am both relieved and excited that it isn't some baby game like making dolls out of sticks, or puppets out of leaves. This seems like a real adventure, something new we have never done before, a real-life treasure hunt.

I read the clue again and know exactly where she is talking about. The place where summer never ends, the place filled with adventure—it could only mean one thing. My favourite place in the whole world. The place where we would go every summer.

Brim's Island.

At breakfast, Nana busies herself around the small kitchen, occasionally placing a plate of toast or juice in front of me but not saying much. Papa isn't here again. He must have left early for work. I haven't seen him for two days, before my birthday, and it feels as though he's avoiding me. Last night I lay awake for as long as I could, waiting for him to come home. When he finally did, I listened as he spoke to Nana in a lowered tone but couldn't make out anything they were saying.

I heard his heavy footsteps coming down the hall, and my heart skipped a beat as he slowed down outside my door, waiting for him to come in. But then his footsteps continued down the hall to his room and the door closed. I had turned away from the door, pulling the sheets up to my chin, and fought the tears back.

Now it's the next morning and he's still not here, and now my heart feels heavy, even though Mama's letters are exciting. Not seeing Papa here for another day, not even to say a belated happy birthday, hurts, and the porridge sticks in my throat.

"The porridge good?" Nana asks, turning from the sink, her fist against her hip.

I nod. "Yes, Nana."

"It's not too hot?"

"No, Nana."

"Hmmm." She turns her back to me, sinking her hands into the sink filled with soapy water.

I know what she's doing. She wants me to tell her about the letters, and normally I would tease her and play along, but all I can think about is Papa missing another birthday.

"Your papa wanted to wish you happy birthday when he got in, but you were asleep," she says, as if reading my mind.

I don't look up, staring intensely at the bowl of porridge as if it were the most interesting thing in the world, but my heart is beating super-fast.

"He says to tell you sorry he missed yesterday. There was some problem at the resort and—"

"It's OK, Nana," I tell her without looking up, and I feel a lump in my throat.

The kitchen falls silent, and I can no longer hear the sound of plates clattering in the sink. When I look up, she is staring at me intently, her eyebrows furrowed, her dark brown eyes soft.

"He didn't mean it, Brie," she says softly. "He never wants to miss your birthday, and it hurt him bad when he does."

I nod the whole time she is talking because somehow the movement of my head seems to delay the tears waiting to fall. I don't know why this upsets me so much every year. I should be used to it by now. This is what Papa does. He makes promises he never keeps.

Nana sighs and shakes her head. "It's not easy for him, Brie," she says, turning back to the sink.

My chest tightens and the tears dry. I clench my jaw. All he has to do is be there for me. Why is that so difficult? Mama did it, and she made it look so easy. Why can't he do it? Is it because I'm hard to look after? Doesn't he like me? My hand tightens around my spoon, and I no longer have an appetite. I stare at the lumps in the porridge that Nana likes so much but I hate.

Sometimes I wonder, if Papa could choose, would he prefer Mama were here instead of me? Maybe it would be easier for him; maybe he would be happier. Maybe he would spend less time at work. My throat hurts just thinking about it.

4

Femi and Smiley find me sitting on the front steps after breakfast. The letter is in my hand, and I'm still thinking about Papa when they let themselves in through the front gate.

The more I think about Papa not wanting me here, the worse I feel, and the less I am excited about Mama's letters.

"What are we doing today?" Smiley asks, sitting next to me on the step. "I say we go to the beach." She fans herself. "Your papa will be down there. He can get us free drinks."

When I don't answer, Femi looks at me, concerned.

"You all right?" she asks quietly.

Femi is good like that. She can always sense when something is wrong, no matter how much you try to hide it. I think that's because she's used to looking after her younger sister, which is forcing her to grow up, so she is always the more mature out of the three of us. The serious one. You have to work really hard to get Femi to act like a kid, but when you do, it feels like you have solved a puzzle no one else could solve.

But what I love most about Femi is how caring she is. When Mama died, she never left my side. She and Smiley stayed at our house for the first few days, but Femi stayed for a whole week. Even when I was excused from school, she would get up, go to school, and come straight back to my house. Femi never says much, but it's always what she does that matters the most. Today I feel her slip her hand into my mine.

"The letters?" she quizzes me.

I shake my head.

She frowns. "Your papa?"

When I don't answer, she nods as if to say she understands. She doesn't ask me anything else; she doesn't need to.

"My papa is always telling me what to do," Smiley chimes in. "Have you cleaned your room? You wash the dishes. You do your homework," she mimics him in a high-pitched voice, turning her lips upward.

I run my fingers along the letter. I want to tell Smiley it's not the same. That I would love for Papa to tell me those things; at least it would mean he was at home long enough to notice.

Femi nods to the letter in my hand. "From your mum?" she asks, leaning her head on me. I nod and Smiley comes to sit on the other side of me.

"What did she say?"

I hand them the letter. "She wants Papa to take me to find some secret she has."

"Ooh," Smiley cries excitedly, scanning the letter. She frowns as it hits her. "So no beach today? I'm so hot."

Femi reads the letter. "Does this mean you're leaving us?"

I shake my head. "I won't be going anywhere, not if Papa is involved."

*

At the resort, Femi and Smiley and I sit on one of the tables on the outside patio. Sheila brings us a bowl of crisps and drinks, so I ask her if she's seen Papa.

"Last I heard, he was in the office," she says, nodding towards the building behind us.

I leave my friends to eat while I walk through reception and down a corridor that is the length of the building. There are three doors, all for staff, and at the end is Papa's office.

I knock on the door and my chest feels funny. Like I've done something wrong and I'm about to face him. I've thought long and hard about whether to ask Papa to take me to Brim's.

Even though Mama said he is the one who will take me, part of me doesn't want to go anywhere with him because I'm so mad at him for missing my birthday, but another part of me is desperate to follow Mama's clues. I'm excited to find out what the secret is, and that is what makes me knock on Papa's office door.

"Come in." His familiar, growly voice barely comes through to the other side of the door.

I open the door, and Papa is sitting behind a dark wood desk that is chipped and peeling. He's always moaning about how the owners won't give him any money to buy new furniture or for a lick of paint to spruce up the place, and how tourists are going to get sick of it and go somewhere else.

He's on the phone, but he gestures for me to sit down in the chair opposite him. He's wearing the usual uniform for this resort, white short-sleeved shirt and dark blue trousers. He already looks tired even though it's still morning, and the lines in his face seem deeper than the last time I saw him.

I sit in the hard-backed brown chair and wait, swinging my legs back and forth. The window behind him looks out onto the public toilets, which hide the sun, making Papa's office dark like the desk and his chair. I wonder why he never demands a better room to work in; it might help with his mood. Make him more relaxed, less intense.

I swing the chair around so I don't have to look at him. Looking at his face only reminds me that he missed my birthday again.

Instead, I find anything else to look at around the room. It's been a while since I've been in here, but nothing has changed. He still has all his certificates on the wall saying how great he is at his job and certificates saying visitors voted it the best hotel, three years in a row.

Next to the certificates is a photo of Papa shaking hands with the boss. A man named Andre who lives in Kingston but rarely visits. Papa looks proud in that picture. His chest is sticking out. He has one leg in front of the other with a slight tilt to his hips. He talks about that day all the time, telling Nana how Andre said he was the best resort resort manager he's ever had and how no one works harder than Papa.

There are two large filing cabinets against the wall, and on top of one of them is a photo of us. Me, him, Mama. It's a photo of when I was born. Mama is cradling me in her arms and Papa is beside her with his arm around her. They are standing in front of a house I don't recognize, and they look happy. Happier than I've seen Papa in a while. Happier than the photo with Andre, his boss. I'm always surprised when I see Papa happy in photos. It's like another life that I can barely remember.

"What's up?" he says, breaking me away from the picture.

I turn in the chair. He doesn't look anything like the guy in the picture now. He's older, less hair; still has his tight curls but now you can see his scalp like his hair is a mirror.

"Brie, I'm sorry I couldn't make your birthday," he says before I have time to speak. "Things got hectic here. You know how it gets—you think you're coming here for a few hours and before you know it you've been here all day." He sits forward with his hands on the desk and his eyebrows furrowed. "You all right?"

I nod, trying not to think about what used to be. How he seemed happier when Mama was here. How she could make him laugh until he held his sides, shouting, "Stop, I can't breathe." How I haven't seen him like that since. How I can barely get him to smile, never mind laugh. How loving me seems to be so hard for him. Like the hardest job in the world.

I swallow all those thoughts and try to focus on why I am here. I don't want to make him mad by bringing up my birthday. I don't want to make things worse when it's already so bad. I want to focus on Mama's letters and go to the one place that made me happy, but to do that, I need him, and that is the hardest part in all of this. Not solving the clues, not figuring out Mama's secret. The hardest part is getting Papa to take me to Brim's Island, and it shouldn't be this hard, but it is.

I take the crumpled letter out of my back pocket and show it to him.

He takes it from me and sits back in his chair reading it. My heart is pounding as I watch his eyes skimming the page. I wait impatiently as he reads it, my heart quickening, hoping that maybe he won't let me down if he knows it's from Mama.

"I would expect nothing else from your mother," he says as he finishes reading it. He drops the letter to his desk, and it floats for a second like a feather before landing lightly on a pile of other papers. He leans further back in the chair, so it tilts and makes a squeaking sound.

My mouth moves from side to side, my hands entwining as I wait anxiously for his answer. In my head I beg him not to let me down, not again.

He rubs his face with his hands, and I wait for what I know is coming. I just wish he would get on with it.

"I just can't right now," he says, shaking his head, and I am already on my feet.

I grab the letter and force a smile. "OK," I say in a stilted voice. I head for the door, but my feet feel stiff, and my arms swing robotically.

"Brie," he calls after me, "I haven't finished."

I turn, fixing a forced smile, so he doesn't see what I am feeling inside.

"These letters are important," he starts, and I can almost predict what he's going to say next. He's going to tell me Mama did a great thing.

"What your mother has done is wonderful. This is a great thing."

Now he will tell me that he can't take me, because of work.

"But it's a busy time for work. I can't afford to drop everything, not right now. I'm so sorry, Brie. I want to, I really do."

I nod as he speaks, and he stops to look at me, frowning.

"We'll do it another time," he suggests. "I'll take some time off later in the year, when it's not so busy, and we'll solve these clues together, you and me. What do you think?"

I think you suck. I think you're always letting me down. I sometimes think that if I ran away, you would never notice. You wouldn't even care.

"Let's pencil in a time," he says, opening his diary. The phone on his desk starts to ring and he hesitates, glancing at it, then at me. "We'll do it tonight, when I get home," he says, and he's already picking up the phone.

I clench my jaw and nod that same robotic nod and open the door and leave, closing it behind me.

5

I find Femi and Smiley on their second bowl of crisps. "You coming, or you going to eat all day?" I say sharply.

They look up at me and Femi frowns.

"What's wrong with you?"

I turn on my heels. "I'm going home. You can come if you want." I walk away, wanting to get as far away from Papa's work as I can so I can forget how he didn't want to spend any time with me. How he couldn't even do the one thing Mama asked him to do. How he let me down, yet again.

At home, I take my phone over to the sofa and sink in it next to Femi, who is deep in a book already.

Smiley sits across from me in Nana's favourite chair, her chin resting on her hands.

"So, your papa won't do it?" she says, frowning.

I shake my head, tapping my phone furiously.

"So what's the plan?" she asks.

I put my phone on speaker and place it on my knee. It rings a few times before it's picked up.

"Hello?" Aunty Elsa's welcome voice comes through the phone, and I lean back in the sofa with my feet under me.

"Aunty Elsa, it's Brie." I tell her about the letter from Mama, how she has some clues that will lead to something special for me.

"And you think it's at Brim's Island?" she asks.

I know it's there. I knew as soon as I read Mama's clue. There is only one place we would go every summer. The only place where we were always together as one family. When all we did was laugh. It was my happy place.

"Papa won't take me," I explain under the watchful eye of Smiley and the odd glance from Femi.

Aunty Elsa sighs on the other end of the line and repeats what I'm saying to an inquisitive Julius. "I'm sorry, Brie," she says, and I feel a lump in my throat.

I had held it together this long, but somehow Aunty Elsa saying nice things makes me want to cry. Maybe I'm more upset about Papa than I realize, or maybe it's the letters from Mama.

"Well, Julius and I wouldn't mind a trip," she says. "I'll see what I can do."

Julius's voice bellows in the background, "Operation Get Brie to Brim's Island is under way."

"Can we come too?" Smiley shouts across the room, but Aunty Elsa has already hung up the phone.

*

"So, you want me to not turn up for work tomorrow?" Papa says into the phone as he hangs his work jacket over the back of the door. He had barely stepped into the house when Nana handed him the phone.

"Elsa wants to talk to you," she had said.

Papa looked tired when he took the phone from her. More tired than when I had seen him this morning, and I feel nervous as he moves from the living room to the kitchen with the phone to his ear.

Femi and Smiley are staying the night, and the three of us sit on the cold, tiled floor in the hallway. We hide behind the wall that separates the living room and the hallway, eating leftover birthday cake in a round silver tin hovering on my lap.

We peer around the wall, listening as Elsa tries to convince Papa to take me to Grandpa Brim's Island, Mama's childhood home.

"You think your papa will let you go?" Femi says, folding her legs under her and filling her mouth with cake.

"Will he let us go too?" Smiley asks with hope in her voice.

All three of us lean around the wall again and try to listen. I don't answer either of them because they know as much as I do—Papa already told me once that he can't go. I don't know what Elsa could say to change his mind.

Papa is now sitting at the table with his usual hot cocoa and bun and cheese. He places the phone on the table and presses the speakerphone.

"You have to lighten up, Winston," Uncle Julius is saying. "You too old to be this grumpy. Life a pass yuh by and what you have to show for it? Work? What else?"

Papa shoots a look at Nana from across the tiny kitchen. I cringe knowing he won't like that. Julius could ruin our chance.

Papa never did like Julius. They are totally different. He is serious, while Julius is fun. Papa rarely laughs while Julius is always laughing. Papa says Julius acts like a pickney, and he needs to grow up. But he only ever says this when Julius isn't around.

"What time she have to be there?" Papa asks, rubbing his face tiredly.

"Why don't you ask Brie?" Aunty Elsa says into the phone. "It's her that this is for."

I am so surprised to see Papa even listening to Julius that I sit up suddenly, toppling the tin to the ground. The sound of it hitting the tiles echoes throughout the house and it lands facedown, throwing the cake everywhere. We freeze, staring at each other, our eyes wide with fright.

"Bridgette, that you?" Papa calls from the kitchen.

"She still awake?" Nana adds in despair. "Mek me go see."

We jump to our feet and run to my room, only to remember the splattered cake on the floor.

"The cake!" I hiss, running back to grab the tin.

Smiley and Femi try to help by scooping the mess back into the bowl. We get as much as we can before running back into the room and closing the door quietly.

I slip the bowl under the bed and the three of us jump under the covers just as the door opens.

Nana sticks her head around the door. "I know you not sleeping so stop the pretending," she says from the doorway.

We don't move, our eyes squeezed tightly shut, holding our breath.

"Smiley's foot in Femi's nose so I know you can't sleep with her stinky feet up there," she declares.

We dissolve into peals of laughter.

"Hmm." She closes the door. "And you can clean up these crumbs before the ants get them," she shouts from down the hall.

*

It's Smiley's idea to do the sign. Smiley likes things like that. She is always the one volunteering to create announcements for school. On Independence Day, she designed a five-foot poster at home and brought it into school to place in the hall. Ms Henderson, our headmistress, was always calling her to write notices for the notice board. I think that maybe if our art teacher was any good, Smiley would see that's what she's good at, but she has no one to tell her that but me.

"We make a sign and have a protest," she suggests that morning.

Femi isn't so sure. "But what are we protesting?"

"Not going on Brie's adventure," she answers. "Adults like visual things like that, and they like to see effort."

I glance at her, knowing full well that's what her parents tell her all the time. Smiley isn't great at academics, but she is good at creating things. Her parents never see that, though; all they see is her grade and tell her to put in more effort.

"OK," I agree.

Femi frowns at me but I ignore her. It's not that I think a sign will convince Papa. I know Papa will say no—he always says no to me—but I know Smiley wants to do the sign. I know it makes her happy, so I throw them a few marker pens and dig around for some paper.

WE, BRIDGETTE, SMILEY AND FEMI, HAVE THE RIGHT TO THE TRIP OF A LIFETIME. THESE ARE OUR REASONS WHY.

We enter the kitchen holding the sign, still bleary-eyed from not enough sleep. We had set our alarms to catch Papa before he left for work. We aren't sure how convincing Aunty Elsa and Julius were last night, but Smiley had encouraged me not to give up, to instead try a different way.

When we enter the kitchen, Papa is already eating his porridge, with his cup of tea beside him and two slices of hard dough bread. Just as I expected, he is dressed for work, although I was hoping he would surprise me and be in his normal clothes ready to drive to Brim's Island.

"Stick to the plan," Smiley says under her breath when she sees me waver.

"What is this?" Nana says, nodding to the pieces of paper in Smiley's and Femi's hands. I feel Smiley nudge me to start.

"Here are the reasons why you should take me to Grandpa Brim's," I announce.

Femi holds up a sign that says #*1*.

"Point number one is that it was all in the letter," I say in my loudest, clearest voice, the one teachers tell you to use when you're speaking at the front of the class even though you're shaking in your shoes and wish you had called in sick. "The letter says to get your father to take you to the place where summer was always an adventure. It says my father, not Nana, or Aunty Elsa or Julius. You.

"Point number two," I say, and my voice wavers a little. I hope he doesn't let me down in front of my friends or get mad that I'm challenging him. I turn to Smiley, who lifts a card that has #*2* on it.

"I have produced perfect grades"—Papa shoots me a look, and I clear my throat—"good grades, and I have been a perfect student. I do my homework on time and have tried out every sport at school for you, Papa."

He drops his spoon in the bowl of porridge and leans back in his chair, which is never a good sign.

"Move on," Femi hisses.

"Point three is we used to do these trips every summer." My voice quiets, and I bite the feelings down. "We had so much fun, driving there, and it

65

will be even better if Femi and Smiley can come, they really make everything better, and back then, when we used to go to Grandpa's house, it was the best time of my life, and I haven't had anything like that for a long time so... that's all I have to say." I can feel my heart pounding hard against my chest and I wonder if they can hear it, too, it's so loud.

"Are you done?" Papa asks, breaking the silence.

I look up and see his arms are folded against his chest. My heart falls, knowing what that means. I nod with a sigh. "Yes, I'm done."

"Good," he says, "because you're leaving tomorrow."

I stare at him blankly and I think I might have stopped breathing.

"We talked last night. Not just us but your parents too," he says to Smiley and Femi.

I feel Smiley grab my hand.

"It was Elsa who suggested bringing your friends along."

My eyes widen and I stare at him in disbelief. "We're going?"

He nods in that barely noticeable way Papa does. "Who am I to argue with your mother?" he says. "If she says you go on a trip, then you go on a trip."

6

Papa tells us that there is so much to do while we all eat breakfast around the small round table in the kitchen.

"I'll help with anything," Smiley volunteers, and Papa nods, pointing at her with his fork.

"That's the spirit," he says, and Smiley beams. He glances at me across the table with a little grin. "If only Brie was as hard working."

Smiley laughs but gets a kick under the table from Femi. I lower my eyes to the plate in front of me and my heart sinks. It's been less than an hour since Papa agreed to take me to Brim's, and already I'm wondering if it's worth it if he's going to make fun of me.

"Brie's always helping out in class," Femi says. "Ms Glen doesn't even have to ask; Brie just does it."

"Does she?" he says, and there is a glint in his eye.

"I've never heard that," Nana says, frowning. "How come you don't tell us these things, Brie?"

"That's what I want to know," Papa agrees.

I shrug, avoiding their eyes. "Didn't think you would care." The words slip out and I clamp my mouth shut. I glance over at Papa and his smile has faded.

Nana's face tightens. "Why would you think that, Brie?"

I wish I could tell them what I'm really thinking without worrying about getting in trouble. I wish I could tell them that ever since Mama died, I feel forgotten. That I go to school and come home, and they ask the same questions without really listening for an answer, so I stopped telling them anything. I wish I could tell them that sometimes I prefer to be at school rather than here because at school the teachers see me. I am not invisible.

Papa clears his throat but there is a heaviness to his voice. "So I take it you're sure of where we're going, because we don't know what the clues mean."

I screw my eyes at him. "You don't recognize the clues in the letter, Papa? The place filled with adventure? The island of fairy tales?"

Papa frowns, his eyebrows furrowed. He turns to Nana and they both shake their heads blankly. "Sounds like something out of a book," he says.

"Brie is sure it's Brim's Island," Smiley says.

His face lights up. "Ah, yes, now it makes sense." He nods, taking a bite of his green banana.

I look at him suspiciously, not sure if he's pretending not to know or if he really doesn't get Mama's clues. I glance at Nana with a cup of tea in her hand; she looks completely clueless, but Papa, I'm not so sure.

"Well, we're going to need a vehicle to carry everyone," he says, "so I'm thinking I should take a quick trip to see Jackfruit after breakfast."

"No work?" I ask, surprised.

He shakes his head. "No work, just us."

I feel a small piece of hope, that this is true, and I finally get to spend some time with him.

Papa starts the short walk out of the complex towards Jackfruit's place. Jackfruit is the town mechanic as well as the tour guide, known by everyone inside the resort and in the nearby town. He owns the local garage, but more than that, he drives the only bus in the resort. Jackfruit's bus is old and creaky. Like the ones you see tourists in because someone told them it was authentic. The kind of buses painted green, yellow and black, all the colours of the Jamaican flag, with *One Love* written on the side in big balloon letters. Once a week, Jackfruit takes all the new tourists on an authentic tour of the island.

When he's not driving his bus, or looking after his garage, Jackfruit is cooking jerk chicken on the street side in an old peeling drum, and he will tell stories of the tourists he meets on his authentic Jamaican bus.

I tag along with Smiley and Femi because I'm excited to have Papa around. I keep expecting his phone to ring and ruin everything, but it doesn't ring, and he doesn't leave.

Papa walks ahead of us along the paved road that sees more people walking than driving, passing villas on either side. Every time he puts his hands in his pockets, I tense, waiting for the call.

"Good morning, Mr Colton."

I recognize the shrill voice of Jill, the woman who lives on the corner of our road. She's in front of us with a towel over her shoulder. Her two kids trail behind, stopping when she stops with heavy sighs, like she's forcing them to do something they don't want to do.

Papa exchanges polite conversation with her, and we wait impatiently to continue out of the complex to see Jackfruit.

"Off to the beach, I assume?" Papa says, nodding towards their towels.

Jill nods, looking over at her two bored kids.

"Yes, it seems the easiest way to keep them amused," Jill says. "Then I can read my book."

"Not bored already, are they?" Papa says, surprised.

"I'm afraid so. Kids these days, eh? What can we do?" She glances over at me and her face changes. "But you're doing so well with yours. She's turned out so well, considering."

My back tenses and I fold my arms across my chest.

Papa glances back but doesn't look at me. He clears his throat. "Er... yes... thank you... She's a good girl."

Jill smiles, nodding. "Yes, she is. She is a testament to you and your late wife, God rest her soul."

Papa shifts his feet, looking away while I glare at her as hard as I can, hoping she will get the message, to stop talking about me like I'm not here. Like I'm some doll that needs fixing.

Papa clears his throat again. "Well, we better be going."

"Oh," she says, her voice short in her surprise. "Anywhere nice?"

I turn my glare to the back of Papa's head, begging him not to tell this nosy woman anything.

"Just seeing Jackfruit," he says, walking away. "Have a good day at the beach, and have a glass of wine on me. Tell Silas at the bar that I sent you."

"Oh you're too kind," she cries as we hurry away before she starts following us.

We hear Jackfruit before we see him, singing at the top of his voice, and then we smell the waft of jerk chicken as he prepares food for the day. Smoke billows from his makeshift cooker, and he rocks from side to side to Beres Hammond, his favourite artist. He is wearing a yellow and black knitted beanie covering his locs. He has a long grey beard that he twists at the end and he's wearing his Chicago vest, which is too big for him, and a long pair of dark jean shorts, his usual clothes that he wears every day.

As we approach, Jackfruit acknowledges Papa with a fist pump and a "Wha' 'appen, brethren."

He turns the chicken over and it makes a loud sizzling sound, sending a new boost of smoke in the air, which makes Jackfruit's eyes water. He steps back, wafting the smoke away.

Papa tells Jackfruit about our trip while he tries to gain control of the fire. He tells him about the letters I got for my birthday from Mama as though he was there, when he wasn't.

Jackfruit squints at me through the smoke. "A true?" he asks me.

I nod to verify the story is true.

Jackfruit nods in approval, sticking the chicken with a long silver fork. "Your mother was always good at them tings," he says. "You know she did organize that party for me and I did never know? You remember?"

Papa nods while shielding his eyes from the piercing sun.

"Got all my friends, even the ones from back home. How she even find dem? You know?"

Papa said he didn't know how she found all his friends, but that Mama was good at things like that.

She knew everyone. Jackfruit agrees. I feel a knot in my throat again, and I'm starting to get frustrated with myself that I can't seem to hear her name without feeling like this.

I'm mad that it still feels like yesterday when it's been three years. I remember at the funeral, people patted me on the head and told me the pain wouldn't last. "It will get easier," they said, but I'm not sure if that's true or if you just push it down so you don't think about it any more.

Silence falls over us that is interrupted only by Jackfruit's food and his apprentice behind us banging underneath a car.

"So, we need a vehicle," Papa says, trying to steer the conversation back. You have to keep it short or Jackfruit will go on for ever about anything and he has a story about everything. "Can we borrow the bus? I heard you only use it on Wednesdays, and we'll have it back before then."

Jackfruit squints at him. "Who tell you that?"

Papa doesn't answer; he already knows Jackfruit might use it as an excuse to keep talking. Jackfruit turns the chicken over and over, occasionally swatting the smoke away.

"We will pay you," Papa says, sweat dripping from his forehead. It's stifling hot the more inland you go, and Jackfruit is away from the beach and the sea breeze. "How much to hire the bus for three days?" He wipes his face with a rag.

Jackfruit rolls his lips from side to side. "It's not the money for me, boss," he says, resting one hand on his hip and squinting over at his bus parked on the gravel outside his garage. "It's my baby, you know? I don't let anyone have it, not even to clean it. Everything I do myself."

Papa nods patiently, taking out his wallet.

Jackfruit eyes Papa leafing through notes of cash. "It's the sentiment for me, you know?" he says, staring at the money. "If anything happen to her, it's not just work I lose, it's family."

Papa glances up from his wallet to make sure he heard right. Jackfruit called his bus family.

Jackfruit notices, his eyes briefly leaving Papa's wallet. "Yes, man," he says adamantly. "It's my family dat. She all I have. I don't know if I can let her go, you know?"

Papa takes out some cash and offers it to Jackfruit, who lingers on it, then sighs.

"But three days is not too long," he says, taking the cash. He stuffs the money under his hat. Before Papa can say anything else, Jackfruit is already sizzling his jerk chicken and singing at the top of his voice.

7

There is a knock on my door, and it opens before I can say anything. Nana peers in.

"Oh, you awake," she says, and comes in, closing the door behind her. She walks to my bed and sits down on the edge. She is wearing what I call her nightie dress. It's a flowery dress that reaches her knees but looks like a hospital gown, it's so big on her. She looks down at me as I scroll through my phone.

"You all right?" she asks gently.

I don't look up from my phone because I feel weird when Nana is like this.

She takes the phone from me. "Let me talk to you for a little bit."

I slide down the bed with my hand on my head, pretending to pass out without my mobile.

"Brie, stop your foolishness." Her voice is impatient, so I stop throwing myself around and push myself up to sitting. Her voice softens again. "It's been a funny few days for you, and I wanted to see how you're doing, you know, since the letters."

I stare at my fingers, suddenly realizing how dirty my nails are. "The trip will be fun," I say, shrugging.

She nods slowly. "Yes, the trip will be good, but is there anything you want to talk about?"

I shake my head.

"Nothing?" Nana asks again, and she sounds a little disappointed.

I shake my head again. "What's for breakfast?" I ask, changing the subject.

She takes a deep breath and pats my legs under the sheets. "You can come and look," she says, her voice returning to its usual breeziness. "You got legs, don't you?"

After she leaves, I listen for her footsteps to get fainter down the hall, followed by the clatter of pans in the kitchen. I feel around under my pillow and pull out the letter. It's a little creased from me lying on it, and the top of the page is bent back, so I try to flatten it.

Then I open it and read it again.

*

I find Nana in the kitchen, cooking away over the white stove. She takes the boiled banana out of the pan and spoons the callaloo into a bowl. I creep up behind her just as she turns with the bowl in her hand. She stops with a start when she sees me.

"You trying to give me a heart attack!" she cries, and I wrap my arms around her waist and hug her. She feels warm and cosy. She lays the pan down on the counter and wraps her arms around me. She kisses me on the forehead but says nothing, just holds me.

We are interrupted by a loud bang on the front door. Nana and I pull apart.

"What is that noise?" Nana cries, annoyed, as the banging continues.

I follow her out of the kitchen and towards the front door.

"Stop breaking my door down," Nana shouts in

her gravelly voice. She yanks the door open and Julius bursts in.

"Surprise!" He does a little dance with his legs bent and arms out in front of him.

Aunty Elsa follows him in, shaking her head but laughing at the same time, and my heart suddenly feels like it's bursting.

Julius lifts me up in a hug and spins me around until I get dizzy. Then he tries to do some handshake that he probably saw on the internet that he thinks all the kids do. He laughs as we fumble, then hugs me again.

Aunty Elsa takes her turn to hug me.

I finally speak. "What are you doing here?"

"We're here to take you to the house," she says. "Didn't your father tell you?"

I nod, confused. "Yes, but he was going to drive us there. He hired Jackfruit's bus."

They exchange looks and I can see Nana lowering her head in the background.

Elsa strokes my face. "Your father isn't coming, Brie. He hired the bus for us, so we could fit everyone in."

I feel my heart fall to the pit of my stomach. This can't be. Not again. I thought he was coming. I was sure he was coming.

The adults talk among themselves about the schedule and the bus and packing, but as they move around me, I stand in the middle of the room, rooted to the floor. This is my father's way of saying that he doesn't want to spend time with me. That work is more important than me. I always thought he felt that way, but now I know for sure.

Jackfruit arrives at 10.45 a.m. with his hand on the horn, which sounds like a ship going out to sea.

Old-time reggae blasts from a battered stereo and black smoke billows from the exhaust.

"You sure this thing can make it?" Nana asks Jackfruit as he climbs out of the bus.

His lips press into a thin line. "Why would you say that, Nanny?" he says with his hand on his chest. Jackfruit always calls her Nanny even though they aren't related and he's too old to be her grandson.

He shakes his head, calling Julius over to go through the rules with him, showing Julius around the bus. I sit on the front step of the house with my bags beside me and Mama's box of letters on my lap. I try to get excited about this trip to Brim's, but all

I can think about is Papa choosing work over me and suddenly I don't want to go on this trip any more. I don't want to go anywhere.

I think of the summers going to Brim's when Mama was here. The excitement the night before. Waking up early and running into Mama and Papa's room, jumping on their bed. Papa would come with us—not for the entire summer, but he came.

I woke up this morning feeling a pinch of excitement, like I used to, but now I don't care if we don't go. I would rather sit in my room in the dark, staring at a blank wall than go on this trip now.

"No, no, no," Jackfruit cries when I try to climb on the bus to get away from everyone. "Yuh can't do that, man. You can't just get on the bus before I finish with the safety rules dem."

Julius peers from behind Jackfruit and shakes his head at me comically, copying Jackfruit.

"I just want to sit down," I tell him.

He shakes his head. "No, Ms Brie, you have to come off the bus until I finish with the safety procedures. My bus, my rules."

I shake my head, annoyed, and get off his precious bus. The bus is too old and stinky for him to be carrying on this way. Anyone would think he had a limousine or something. I throw him a glare as he continues to take Julius around the bus.

"Brie, help me put these bags in the back," Aunty Elsa calls.

I begrudgingly drag my feet around the bus to the back where Femi and Smiley are helping.

"All of us?" I say, irritated.

Aunty Elsa stands straight and raises her eyebrows. "What, you too good to lift bags?"

I shake my head, more to myself than to her, and pick up someone's small suitcase and throw it into the long, dusty luggage hold.

When all the bags are in, we head around the bus where Julius is calling us to get on. I feel Aunty Elsa's arm on my shoulder from behind. She moves beside me, matching my step.

"Your father has a business to keep running. Sometimes adults need to do things you won't always like. It doesn't mean he didn't want to come."

She tilts her head to look at me as we reach the steps of the bus. "You hear me, Brie?" she says gently in my ear.

"Mama said he should take me," I say quietly,

and climb onto the bus. I find a seat at the back of the bus away from everyone, placing her box on my lap. I wish adults would stop making excuses for each other when they do something wrong. When I do something wrong, I get punished for it, yet the rules are always different when you're grown. Mama didn't say I should go with Elsa, or Julius, or the entire town. She said Papa and so Papa has let me down.

Unlike Mama, who found it easy to say and show how she felt, Papa is quiet, strict and only cares about how good I am at school.

All he ever asks me is did I listen to the teachers, did I do my homework, did I try out for the football team. He doesn't hug me the way Mama would have when I won the spelling bee or when I made the netball team. She would have pulled me to my feet and embarrassed me by swinging me around, squealing at the top of her voice, no matter where we were. But at least she cared. At least she would have been on this bus.

Jackfruit gets on the bus with a notepad and pen and announces he needs to make a note of how many people are here.

Julius, who is now behind the wheel, turns in his seat. "I got it, my man," he says, but Jackfruit shakes his head.

"When I call out your name, then raise your hand."

Nana, who is sitting at the front of the bus, kisses her teeth impatiently. "There's three children and three big people," she snaps at Jackfruit. "Let we get on our way. Mi too hot for dis."

"Nanny, I understand yuh concern, but dis is my bus and these are my rules," he says, pointing his pen at her. "I cannot be responsible for losing these pickneys here. My reputation is solid." He glares at her for a second longer than necessary. "Solid," he repeats.

Nana shakes her head and mumbles something to Aunty Elsa behind her, who chuckles, shaking her head.

When we are finally allowed to go, Julius starts the engine and drives away towards the front gate.

8

Julius beeps his horn non-stop as we head down the long, flat road that leads us to the gate where Almond and Prince are sitting in their security box. He turns left out of the resort and away from the beach, along a winding road lined with trees and bushes on either side of us. The bushes soon become houses, and our yellow-bricked school sits back off the road on our left.

We pass more houses, the local supermarket, the hair shop where Mama used to work, and Jackfruit's garage. The road comes to a junction, and Julius turns right onto the main coast road that rolls through the island. He speeds up to try and match the other cars around him, but the bus is too old and too slow, so cars overtake us, honking impatiently.

The sea breeze bathes our faces through the open windows. I look out to the right as the bus rolls beside the low sea wall separating us from the low tide on the other side, wondering where this adventure will take us and what other clues Mama has in her letters.

Mama would always make sure we had three things on our road trip. Food, music and a list of games to play in her head.

I take out my phone and film everyone from the back of the bus. Femi, two seats in front on the left, leaning against the window with her feet up to her chin, engrossed in a book already. Smiley bothering Aunty Elsa about something. I can't tell what because the engine of the bus is so loud it drowns her out.

Nana is already digging into her bag of food.

I turn the camera on myself and throw up a peace sign. "Happy holidays," I tell the camera before shutting it off. But it doesn't feel like it's going to be happy. It feels like we are hurtling towards something I would rather avoid.

*

Three hours later, the bus slows down and enters Bridgetown, the tourist village on the north coast. Mama told me once that way back when, before all the tourists found Bridgetown, it was just a quiet seaside town, but then it got popular when visitors found the long beach that went on for miles and calm blue waters.

Bridgetown is filled with strange-looking tourists who wear hats with dreads hanging out of them and shout "Yea mon" or "irie" to any local they see.

Every time we visited the beach here, it was filled with tourists lying on the long white beach and locals selling them food or braiding their hair. The odd fishing boat would rock under tiny ripples of waves, and every now and then the calm sea was interrupted by a boat filled with foreigners and loud music, but then the sea would fall silent again.

We follow the coastal road as it winds away from the beach and into the hills, taking us scarily close to the edge of the cliff that overlooks the sea with rocks beneath. The footpath disappears as we climb the winding road while tourists in flip-flops and swimsuits navigate the road along with cars and locals. A bus occasionally whizzes dangerously by us with music pumping out of its speakers.

The winding road levels, and the further we drive, the worse the road gets. Eventually as the road flattens way above the sea, Julius stops outside a large multicoloured house. Each brick of the house is painted a different colour. It's built into the rocks with the hidden caves underneath. It sits behind large iron gates to stop nosey strangers from walking in.

Julius stops the bus outside, while Aunty Elsa jumps out and opens the gate to let him in.

He drives in and parks by a large sycamore tree.

"Last stop," Julius announces, climbing out of his seat. "Collect your things and leave nothing behind or the duppy man will tief it in the night."

When everyone is off, Julius leads us to the front door. He slides the key into the lock and turns to us, smiling broadly.

"For those of you who have been before, welcome back." He winks at me. "For those of you who have never been, welcome to Brim's Island."

He opens the door into a world filled with Brim's wildest imagination.

My grandad Brim was well known in Bridgetown. Some called him strange, and others called him a genius. Grandpa Brim had a wild imagination that left you in awe. He could sit for hours telling you stories off the top of his head. Wild, magical stories of talking donkeys that rule a kingdom hidden under his house. He would remember every name from every story he made up, even when you tried to catch him out.

"Grandpa Brim, I thought the lady who sang so she could fly was the queen of the kingdom," I would say, encouraged by Mama.

Brim, who when not telling stories was either planting flowers and plants or adding something new to his house, would shake his head without a beat. "No, that's not what I said. I said she tried to be queen but the songs she sang didn't impress the donkey because the donkey could only hear rap, not reggae," he said, and Mama and I would giggle.

The first room we enter from outside is decorated like back a bush. Grandpa Brim's house is magical, filled with bright colours and strange-shaped furniture. In the living room, the walls are painted in the greens, browns and yellows of the forest. There are trees climbing the walls, their branches exploding across the ceiling. The roof is painted a sunset gold and yellow and red with the moon hiding behind the branch of a tree.

There are four chairs and a round table made from a tree stump, and a long bench used as a sofa, also carved out of a tree and all covered in green and brown cushions that his wife had made, but I never met her; she died before I was born.

The hall that leads to the bedroom and the kitchen at the end is painted like a waterfall. Rocks are drawn into the roof, and the water flows down the walls onto the floor, where Brim has painted a river with bullfrogs jumping.

Julius takes us into the kitchen, where more trees tower above us, climbing up the walls and into the ceiling. Only this time they have birds perching on branches and hummingbirds flying overhead.

I love this place. The adventures we would have with Brim are memories I have shut away and not thought about for a long time. To think of this magical house is to think of Brim, and to think of

Brim is to think of Mama when she didn't have cancer.

Julius chatters non-stop about the house and how it used to be full of life when Brim was around. "It's too quiet now," he says, "and no one appreciates this except me."

Aunty Elsa shoots him a look, shaking her head.

Last year, Aunty Elsa, Julius and Papa decided to put Brim in a home for old people. Brim hadn't been himself for a while. After Mama died, he started to act funny. Forgot people's names, forgot where he lived. Papa said the final straw was when Aunty Elsa got a call from a neighbour saying she had found him in town looking confused. They were scared to leave him alone after that. He didn't have any other family apart from us. Aunty Elsa couldn't stay at home to look after him, and Papa said he couldn't either with work, so they put him in a home five miles away.

No one asked me what I thought. I didn't even get a vote. They told me one day after school, in between homework and dinner.

Julius leads us through the large kitchen, which takes up the entire back of the house, and out into the back garden, where there is nothing but trees surrounding the house. Trees as tall as the sky.

The garden is flat and long, filled with more trees and flowers than you can count on either side. At the bottom, the garden disappears between a forest of trees, and behind the trees is a wall at the edge of the cliff and the sea down below.

We follow Julius down the garden, where pink and red flowers light up our walk.

The garden slopes downward and the trees close in on us, making the garden narrower and the trees seem taller the further down we go. A stony path guides us through the trees, and we follow it to the end. Julius walks over to the trees to the right. He pushes through the nestle of trees and disappears inside.

"Where'd he go?" Smiley gasps.

I smile knowingly and follow him. We emerge through the trees on the other side. Grey stone steps lead down to a tunnel built into the rocks. I have told my friends many times about my adventures when I came here for the summer. But this I have kept a secret. I don't know why; it just felt like something only our family shared. I liked having something that was only ours.

We follow Julius down the stone steps dug into the rocks while he talks non-stop about how nice it is down here, especially at night. His voice echoes in the tunnel, and my friends shout to hear their own voices echoing and laugh hysterically when they echo back.

In front of us, the tunnel opens onto a small cove, and a white sandy beach with the sea floating lazily towards us.

Femi and Smiley look around, taking in everything in awe. I inhale deeply as the sea air wafts around us, and it's as if everything disappears. The letters and not knowing what to think of them or how I should act. Papa, letting me down again. In that moment, all I feel is peace. It's as if the breeze washes everything away.

I turn to face my friends with my arms outstretched and announce: "Welcome to Brim's Island."

9

Brim's Island is what we called Brim's magical house on top of the rocks. What Mama and I called it. It seems the perfect name for something so perfect that Brim built. Brim's Island is so special that big companies would offer him lots of money for it. Brim always refused. "This is my home, and my home is not for sale," he would adamantly tell each of them.

It is the perfect place to be in this moment, and I understand why Mama's letter brought me here. This is where we laughed the loudest. This is where Mama became a kid, excited, and filled with a light that did not fade the entire time we were here. This is where we danced under the moonlight, played catch on the beach and ate fried fish under the stars.

This is where we came to escape. Whatever problems we had when we came here, we always left feeling like nothing mattered.

Smiley wraps her arm around my shoulder.

"This is going to be the best time of our life," she says, and as she pulls away, her eyes are gleaming. "I can feel it."

*

We sit on the wall surrounding the house, our legs dangling off the edge, as we wait for the ice cream man. Peto rides his bike through the neighbourhood with a cooler filled with ice cream and soda. I remember the summers we would come here and Brim would shout, "Ice cream man!" Mama would grab my hand and run out as the sound of the bell on Peto's bike got closer.

Today, though, the road is quiet. Only two cars have passed in the last half hour. Aunty Elsa said he would be here any minute, but it's been thirty minutes and no ice cream man.

"We could have walked to town and got it quicker," Femi moans, throwing her head back, trying to catch some breeze.

"Uncle Julius says he will take us into town later," I say, clicking record on my phone and panning it slowly around to Smiley's face. She sticks her tongue out at the camera.

"Which would you rather," Smiley says, "win the lottery or live for ever?"

"Lottery," Smiley and I say immediately.

"Live for ever," Femi says.

Smiley and I scowl at her.

"Money can't buy you happiness," Femi says.

"Only poor people say that," I scoff.

Femi's mouth falls open. She turns to me in disbelief. "Did you call me poor?"

I nod and give her a pat of sympathy.

"OK, would you rather listen to your parents' old music for one day, or listen to your music every hour for the rest of your life?"

"Our music," we all say in unison, and we laugh because we never agree on anything.

Smiley goes to speak again but Femi nudges me. "Who is that?"

We all turn to where she is looking. A boy around our age is riding towards us on a bike. His wheels are bouncing up and down on the uneven road. His hair is in short dreads that bounce when he pedals. He is wearing a crisp white T-shirt and jean shorts to his knees.

"Who is that?" Smiley repeats as he gets closer, steering the bike with one hand and carrying a plastic bag with the other. As he gets closer, he slows down and stares at me. I glare back at him with wide eyes.

"You need something?" I ask, confused.

He puts his foot down to stop the bike. "Brie?" he says.

I frown at him as he smiles at me.

"It's me, Paulton."

Paulton. Brim's neighbour lives about eight hundred yards down the road. His mama used to be friends with my mama. When Mama and I came to visit in the summer, Paulton and I would play together. I haven't seen him since Mama died three years ago.

He didn't have locs then.

He walks his bike over to us. "What you doing here?" He leans his bike against the wall.

"Spending the summer," I tell him, but I don't tell him about Mama's letters; too many people know about them already.

Smiley jumps off the wall. "I like your bike," she says.

Paulton climbs onto the wall next to me. "You can ride it if you like," he says.

She flushes through her brown skin. "I don't know how to," she says. "Can you show me?"

Paulton jumps down from the wall and walks his bike into the middle of the road. He beckons Smiley over and starts telling her what to do with her arms and legs.

Femi frowns. "Doesn't she have a bike back home?"

I nod—"Yep"—and we watch as she pretends to fall off.

Smiley continues to pretend she's never seen a bike before until the bell of the ice cream man interrupts her. Peto rides towards us and stops when we wave him down. He steps off his bike, leaning it against the wall of Brim's house.

"Chocolate, coconut, rum raisin, pineapple, strawberry, mango, soursop." He reels off the flavours, opening the cooler filled with different tubs.

We shout our flavours, and he grabs the scoop and a cone.

After Peto has gone, Paulton leaves with the bag of shopping he has for his mama. We watch him walking his bike with one hand and licking his ice cream with the other. We head back into the house before our ice cream melts.

"Oh, I don't know how to ride a bike." I mimic Smiley.

"Oh, I don't know how to walk. Can you show me?" Femi joins in, pretending to fall over.

Smiley rolls her eyes. "I really am not good at it, OK?" she says, a smile pulling at her lips.

"No, you're not," Femi says. "Flirting is not your thing. Don't do that ever again. It was embarrassing."

Even Smiley can't help but laugh as we go into the house.

I enter the first bedroom on the left, the room I call my own when I'm here. The room that used to be Mama's. We've changed it a lot over the years. Brim always allowed Mama to decorate her room how she wanted, and Mama did the same for me.

A double bed is set against the wall across from the door, underneath the window. Against the left wall is a white wooden wardrobe and a dresser sits against the opposite side. But it's the walls that make the room. We painted it blue like the sea, adding butterflies, mine and Mama's favourite insect. I had forgotten we had painted the walls on our last visit here. You can tell which butterflies were drawn by me and which ones were drawn by Mama. Mine are sloppy and barely recognizable as butterflies.

We lie on the cold tiled floor, our bare feet up against the wall while we eat our ice cream. The roof fan spins above us, making a whirring sound but providing a welcome breeze.

"So, how long have you known Paulton?" Smiley says casually.

I shrug. "Since we started coming here, when I was three. Next question?"

Smiley pouts. "I was only asking."

"When was the last time you opened one of your mama's letters?" she says, trying to catch her ice cream with her tongue before it melts.

I realize then that I haven't opened Mama's next letter as she asked me to do when I arrived. I got so caught up with showing Femi and Smiley around that I almost forgot about the letters, and I almost forgot about Papa. One always seems to remind me of the other.

I sit up, wiping my mouth with the back of my hand. I crawl over to the bed because I can't be bothered to stand.

"Turn the other way," I tell them.

They turn their heads and I reach under the bed, where I have chosen to hide the box with Mama's letters.

"Why do we have to turn away?" Smiley complains with her eyes shut.

I push the box into the middle of the room, Aunty Elsa's singing echoing down the hall.

"Because if you look before I tell you, the light from the box will explode into the room and you'll disintegrate into a thousand pieces," I tell her, sitting in front of the box and crossing my legs under me. "You can look now. I've unlocked the code and the light has disappeared."

Smiley doesn't find this as funny as Femi.

I open the box to fake gasps from Smiley and Femi.

"What is it?" Smiley cries with her hands on her face. "Is it... a new phone?"

I flash her a sarcastic smile and take out the third and last letter.

I stare at the envelope and her writing, and my chest feels tight again.

"Do you think there will be another clue in there?" Smiley asks, leaning forward to try and read the letter upside down.

This is it. This is the clue that will lead me to Mama's secret. My heart is beating fast as I take out the familiar writing paper and unfold it. I scan the words to try and find the clue, but all I can think about is how once, three years ago, Mama wrote this to me, how her writing seems so real, as though she wrote it an hour ago. How letters can tell you lies, can make you believe that nothing has changed, and everything is still the same.

"Well," Smiley says impatiently, "what does it say?"

I clear my throat and read the letter out loud.

My Dearest Brie,
   If you read this, it is because you have solved the first clue. Well done! You are at the place we all loved so much. I have so many memories of

Brim's Island. So many with you, so many before you. So many stories I meant to share with you but ran out of time.

When my papa first built this house, it was because he had a dream one night, and that is how all his projects began—with a dream. In this one, he saw a house of mystery and adventure. He wanted every room to tell a story. From the colours of the walls to the river on the floor. He created new worlds for me to explore and when the house was finished, he told me a secret.

He said that hidden within this house is a secret door. If I found that door, I got to keep whatever was inside. Can you imagine how excited I was to hear there was a secret door? It made all my adventure dreams come true. It was like the books I had been reading had come to life, in my house.

I spent days searching for the door. Every morning before school, every evening when I got home. But I couldn't find it. Then one day, when I was losing hope, as if by chance, I found it.

My father told me that whatever was behind that door was now mine and he would keep it a secret for as long as I wanted.

When I got sick, I remembered the door that got me through my childhood. The door that was mine, and how much it changed me. How much it made me who I am.

Who I was.

It has been a while since I've seen it, so I don't know what condition it's in, if Brim looked after it, or if he kept to his word and never entered.

But whatever condition it is in, I want to pass it on to you. This is my present to you, Brie, and it will be my present to you for as long as you need it.

To find it, ask my father for the key that unlocks the hidden door. Then you have to find the door the key unlocks.

Love always,
Mama

We all fall silent, and I fold the letter and place it back in the envelope. My heart is beating fast as I lay the letter in the box, and when I finally look at my friends, their eyes are sparkling with excitement, just like mine.

"There's a secret door!" Smiley shouts in disbelief with her hands on her head. She runs around the room opening doors and drawers, shouting, "Where is it? We have to find it."

"That's pretty cool," Femi says, nodding in approval. She looks at me. "Isn't it?"

My head is filled with so many questions. I want to run around the house looking for this door. I want to ask Mama how long she's had this secret and why she didn't tell me. I want to run outside and ask

Aunty Elsa what she knows, but I also want to keep it a secret and find it for myself. I want to phone Papa and tell him but I also don't want him to know anything because he doesn't deserve to know, not after letting me down. I want the girls to help me, but I also want to do it alone.

"It's amazing," I agree, but I'm not sure if I said it to myself or to them. All I can hear is my breathing, loud against my ears as though I've just run a mile.

Then as quickly as the excitement comes, it is replaced by worry.

"It doesn't matter anyway," I tell them, closing the box, deflated. "Brim won't remember my name, never mind knowing where the key to the room is."

10

Later that evening, we sit around two small tables that Elsa brought outside. She lays the tables as though we are in a restaurant. Julius switches on the fairy lights Mama brought here once. She saw it in a magazine and thought it was pretty.

The air is cool at night from the sea below, and I am shivering. I enter the house to find something warm to wear and head to my room.

We used to use that room for storage, so there is always a jacket lying around.

I open the wardrobe door and look inside. Immediately I spot a jacket among the old clothes. It's a long blue jacket that was Mama's. It was her favourite, with white thread sewn through and two big pockets at the front that you can sink your hands into all the way to your wrists.

I run my fingers along the edges, trying to remember what Mama looked like in it. She liked her hair up in a casual bun when she wore it, usually on a cool evening like this one. She would wear loose trousers that swallowed her up, and no make-up. She would sit outside in Brim's wooden chair, one leg up, the other swinging across the floor. She would be laughing loudly at something silly she and Elsa remembered. She had the loudest laugh.

She would invite me to join her, opening the jacket and moving over in the chair to allow me beside her. She would wrap it around me, still talking, still laughing as I cuddled in beside her, resting my head against her chest. I would listen to her heart beating, faster when she laughed, slower when she listened.

I slip the jacket on and let out a sigh, wrapping it around me. I inhale and try to figure out if it still smells like her. If Elsa or Papa washed it since Mama died or if, like me, they wanted to keep every bit of her just as it was before.

When I return to the table, everyone is busy talking. I sit next to Smiley and spoon some rice onto my plate.

Smiley nudges me as I sit down. "Ask them."

I glance across the table at Aunty Elsa and Nana in deep conversation about some television show they both watch. We have an old TV at home that only Mama watched. But every Saturday, Nana lets me watch a movie with her, because she's too engrossed to send me to bed.

"Not now," I tell her under my breath.

"Yes, now," Smiley insists. "We're only here for a few days, Brie, and I don't want to miss all this hidden-door-secret thing." She waves her arms around wildly as she tries to explain herself.

"What's got you so excited?" Aunty Elsa says. She and Nana have stopped talking and now they are looking at Smiley, bemused.

Smiley glances at me and I shake my head.

"Brie's letter said there was a secret door in this house but to find the secret door she needs a key and the only person who knows about the key is her grandad Brim, who might not even remember because... you know," Smiley blurts out without taking a breath. When she finishes, she mouths *Sorry* to me.

Now they're all looking at me.

"Say what?" Julius cries with an amused raise of his eyebrow.

Smiley opens her mouth to repeat, and I stop her with my hand. I shift in my seat.

"Mama said there was something special, behind a door that only she knew about. She said it changed her life and she wanted me to have it." I shrug. "But only Brim has the key and he won't remember, so"—I sigh—"it doesn't matter."

I move the rice around my plate, waiting for them to tell me that it won't work, not if Brim is involved.

"Well, there's only one way to find out," Julius says, and he turns to Elsa for confirmation.

I meet Elsa's eyes and she smiles at me. "Why don't we go and ask him tomorrow. You never know. Brim is full of surprises."

*

"Your grandpa sounds amazing," Smiley says as we settle into bed.

It's a squeeze with the three of us in one bed, so we sleep head to toe. Me and Femi at one end, Smiley at the other.

We fall silent in the dark, and my head is still swirling thinking about Mama's letter and the secret door. I have a funny feeling in the pit of my stomach. Like a mixture of excitement and dread. What if I don't find the door? All this would have been a waste. The letters, the time Mama put into the letters when she was probably at her sickest. The fuss to get me here, Aunty Elsa and Julius coming to get me. I sigh, staring at the ceiling as my eyes adjust to the dark.

"Would you rather eat your own poo for five minutes or eat the same meal for the rest of your life?" Smiley says in the dark, but Femi doesn't answer. Maybe she fell asleep, or maybe like me she's thinking about the secret room.

"Hello?" Smiley says into the dark.

*

The next morning at breakfast, my friends are still talking about Mama's secret door. They seem more excited than I am.

"Maybe it's outside," Smiley suggests between bites of toast.

I squint at her. "Outside?"

She nods. "If I was going to hide something, then I would hide it where no one would think."

"But outside?" I repeat, pulling open my fried dumpling and piling scrambled egg inside.

"Nana, did you know about this door?" Smiley asks Nana.

She shakes her head, leaning back in her chair with a hot tea in her hand. "It's the first I ever heard," she says, bemused.

I glance over at Aunty Elsa, who is listening silently, which isn't like her at all.

"Aunty Elsa, do you know about the door?" I ask her suspiciously.

She shakes her head. "No, I know nothing. All the time I knew your mother, she never said anything, not once."

She and Mama were close, so I guess she must be almost as confused as I am.

Julius appears in the doorway, beaming. "I spoke to the home. They said we can visit Brim this morning."

My head shoots up. "Really?"

He rubs his hands together, then checks his watch. "I said we would be there by ten, so eat up."

"Ten?" Nana says, trying to read the clock in the kitchen. "Why you tell them so early?"

Julius moves around the table to where Nana is sitting and massages her shoulders. "Come on, Nanny," he says. "You can do it. I believe in you."

Nana sighs and takes another sip of her tea. "This doesn't feel like no holiday," she mutters. "This feels like work."

*

"Last man on the bus stinks of donkey doo-doo," Julius shouts in the hall.

We appear from different parts of the house. Femi and Smiley from the bedroom, me from the kitchen. We race to the front door, left wide open by Julius, just in time to see him jump on the bus and stick his tongue out at us. Sometimes I can see what Papa means when he says Julius acts like a pickney. Especially now when he's sticking his tongue out at us through the bus window.

We race outside, around the bus, and climb on, throwing ourselves onto the nearest seat, laughing and catching our breaths.

"Nana, you a stinky doo-doo?" I call out to her as she slowly walks out the door with Aunty Elsa.

She shoots me a glare and I stifle my laugh.

We wait impatiently for them to get on the bus and find their seat.

Julius looks back. "Ready?" he shouts.

"Yes!" Smiley replies.

Julius repeats it again until we all reply in unison, although not as enthusiastically as Smiley.

"Brim, here we come!" He presses on the horn as we pull out of the front yard and turn right down the road.

11

The home where Brim is staying is off the main road about ten minutes away from Brim's Island. A few minutes down a long dirt road and we emerge into an opening with a small one-storey house on the left. Next to it is what looks like a house used as an office. To the right of us is a large garden held in by a fence that surrounds the property.

Julius climbs out of the bus. "Hello?" he calls out a few times before a woman emerges from the house.

She breaks into a smile when she sees him. "Hello, Julius," she says, walking down the steps. "You here to see Mr Harlow?" She peers into the bus. "You bring the entire town?"

Julius laughs his loud, hearty laugh. "No, no, just family," he explains.

She nods. "Well, you will have to leave the bus here. It won't make it any further."

Julius waves us off the bus and we climb down one by one.

"Does he know we're coming?" Aunty Elsa asks worriedly.

The woman lays a reassuring hand on Elsa's arm. "Yes, man," she says. "We told him, and he's been waiting by the window all morning."

We follow Julius along a grassy path with only a few stone markers placed in the ground to show us the way. We pass the house that is being used as an office, and then there is nothing else but towering trees and unkempt grass, until we turn a corner and see the building ahead of us peeking through the trees.

Elderly Village is less a village and more a large, one-storey house painted lime green. It sits at the end of the grassy road among towering trees that darken the home even when the sun is out.

Outside in the large yard, there are a few wooden tables with benches and a wraparound porch with more chairs. The house is quiet, and I remember it being quiet when I came here a month ago to visit Brim. It always makes me worry for Brim, who hates quiet. He likes to do things. He doesn't like being still.

A feeling of dread comes over me as we approach the house. The same feeling I got when I visited him last time. It's as if the house is a person, watching us, waiting to pounce and lock us inside.

We step onto the porch and look around for someone. The white shutters against the windows are open, but it's dark inside.

Julius knocks on the front door. A minute later, it opens and a short woman wearing a blue uniform and her hair gelled back into a small ponytail looks out at us.

"You here to see Brim?" she says, and she opens the door wider to let us in. "Follow me."

We follow her through a dark living room and dining room where the TV buzzes low and two people sit staring at it, their bodies hunched forward, their heads tilted. She takes us down the hall and stops at the end, pointing to an open door.

Julius enters and we follow behind him in a line.

"Brim!" Julius exclaims, but I can't see anything, the room is so small and there are too many of us.

I move around Smiley and Femi, and around Nana to see a brown chair facing the window.

There is a small wooden bed against the wall to the right. A brown chest of drawers to the left has a small TV on top playing fuzzy pictures. I walk over to the chair and around it.

Brim is sitting in the high-back chair, staring out the window, but his eyes are blank.

"Brim," I whisper.

But he doesn't look like the Brim I used to know. He looks older than I've ever seen him, and sick. The sparkle in his eyes has gone and now they are blank. His face is covered in wrinkles, more than I've ever seen on him before, like Mama's wrinkled letter that I carry in my pocket. His full head of curly hair is nearly gone. What's left is completely white. His shoulders are bent forward and he looks small, like an old child.

Something about the way he looks makes my breath catch in my throat. I bite my lip to stop the tears that flood my eyes. I turn to Julius and Aunty Elsa.

"What's wrong with him?"

Aunty Elsa moves over to me and wraps her arm around my shoulder. "He's sick," she says quietly, and her voice falters.

Femi and Smiley sit on Brim's bed while Nana, Aunty Elsa, Julius and I sit or stand around Brim's chair. They talk to Brim about the house, about their work, about the weather and the news, but Brim doesn't say anything back. I sit on the floor by his feet, looking up at him, wondering when he will see us. Or if he even remembers who I am.

Occasionally he comes out of his trance and looks at us blankly, but then he fades away.

After a while, Nana says it's time to go. "We need to pay them for this month too," she says to Julius. Nana follows Julius and Aunty Elsa out and turns when she sees I'm not following. "Come, Brie," she says. "We can come back another time."

"OK," I tell her. "I'm right behind you."

They disappear around the corner.

I get on my knees and tap Brim on the arm. "Brim, get up." I try to pull his arm but he's heavy.

"Brie, what are you doing?" Smiley hisses as my friends watch me from the bed.

"Brim," I say again, more urgently.

He looks up as if hearing me for the first time and his eyes light up.

"Dee?" he says, his voice shaky and filled with surprise. He takes my hand. "Dee, my child, where have you been?"

For a minute I'm frozen to the spot. I don't know what to do. Brim has mistaken Aunty Elsa for Mama before. So I decide to ignore it and continue to pull him to his feet.

"Brie, what are you doing?" Femi echoes Smiley.

I turn to them frantically. "Help me," I say as I hear murmurs of Nana's and Elsa's voices down the hall.

They jump to their feet and rush over.

"Help you do what?" Femi asks, confused.

"Help me get him out."

Both of them stare at me as if they misheard me.

Femi is the first to speak. "Help you do what, Brie?" she says, leaning forward as if that will help her hear better.

I look at Brim, stroking my hand, thinking I am Mama. I wonder whether to tell him that I'm not Mama, or just to do what Aunty Elsa does and play along.

My heart pounds against my chest. I look around frantically, trying to think of what to do. I turn to the window that is already cracked open and push it out as far as it will go. I climb onto the windowsill and peer out. The ground is only a short drop away. Short enough for me to step out. I look back at Brim. My heart is pumping so fast I can barely breathe. A voice in my head is screaming, *Don't do it*. Papa will be so mad, but another voice tells me it's the right thing to do. To save Brim from this prison. That's what Mama would have done. She would be the first to tell me to look out for the nurses while she lifted Brim out the window. Mama would not have left him here and I can feel her around me, telling me it's the right thing to do.

"What are you doing?" Femi asks, horrified. She starts to pace the room. "We're going to be in so much trouble."

I tell her to watch the door while I climb out the window to the ground below. "Bring him to the window," I hiss to Smiley.

They both look at me, mortified.

"Quick!" I shout, suddenly hearing voices coming down the hall.

"Brim." I take him by the shoulder to get his attention. "Remember when you would climb out the window to see your girlfriend? When your mama wouldn't let you?"

His eyes light up again and he nods. "Of course I remember, Dee. I'm old, not senile."

I reach through the window for his hands, and he takes them while climbing through the window unsteadily with the help of Smiley.

"Now what?" Femi hisses from the doorway.

"You need to distract them," I tell her. "Give us enough time to get on the bus."

Femi shakes her head frantically. "Brie, no. I can't get in trouble. I just can't."

I help Brim through the window to the ground.

"You can do it, Femi," I tell her, "please."

She bites her lip, frowning, then nods firmly as if convincing herself and disappears down the hall.

I grab Brim's hand and we run around the back of the house, through the trees until we spot the bus. Standing in front of the bus is Nana, fanning herself while she waits for us.

I turn to Smiley. "You need to distract Nana."

Smiley glances over at Nana, then back at me, her

eyebrows squished together. "I don't know what's happening," she says in an uncertain tone. "Why have we kidnapped your grandad?"

I glare at her. "Because he doesn't belong there. Because he's not living in there. He's dying. He needs to be home, on Brim's Island, where he can feel alive again." I thought out of everybody that Smiley would understand. She is more adventurous than Femi. Always willing to do something daring, always the first to stand up for what's right.

We lock eyes and my heart is pounding so fast my words come out breathless. "Because you have to spend time with people before they're gone and do all the things you should have done before it's too late."

I peer through the trees where Nana is still pacing, then turn back to her. "I need to get him on the bus before they all come back, but I need someone to distract Nana. Are you in or not?"

Smiley's face softens. "OK," she says quietly, "I'll do it."

Before I can tell her what to say to Nana, she pushes through the bushes and runs towards the bus, waving at Nana to get her attention. I kneel down behind the bushes and watch as she starts talking to Nana and pointing towards the home. My knees feel unsteady, and breaking the rules doesn't seem as fun without Mama. I'm scared. Scared of doing something that will hurt Brim, scared of Papa finding out and sending me home, scared of not finding Mama's secret door. I take a deep breath and try to push those thoughts to one side. I'm here now. There's no turning back. I have to finish this. I inhale deeply and turn to Brim.

"Brim, we're going to—"

"Run to the bus and get on the bus and hide," he says to my surprised face. "I'm old, Dee, not deaf. You pickneys been talking over me like I can't hear a word you saying."

"But can you run fast?" I tease him, hoping it will trigger his memory of us, racing along Brim's beach. Him on my heel giving me a lead and shouting, "But can you run fast?" as he catches up with me.

Brim looks me up and down in disgust. "I bet I can run faster than you," he scoffs.

I smile, laying my arm on his shoulder, and it's the small relief I need to stop my nerves from getting the better of me.

Smiley walks Nana away from the bus and she waves her hand behind her as the signal.

"Go, go, go," I hiss, grabbing Brim's hand as we run out into the open and around the back of the bus. I peer around the corner to check it's clear, then run alongside the bus, gripping Brim's hand tightly. I help him on the bus before Nana notices. We crawl to the back, where I tell Brim to lie down on the seat and hide.

I sit in front of him; my heart pounding not knowing if this will work. Smiley gets on the bus and gives me a darting gaze, then looks around. As she gets to the back of the bus, she spots Brim lying down. She sits stiffly in the seat opposite me, staring straight ahead.

"Is this going to work?" she asks.

I'm about to answer when I spot Julius and Elsa coming back with Femi.

I feel sick to my stomach as they get closer. I peer behind me, where Brim is lying on the seat. I don't know if it's going to work. I don't know if we're going to get away with this. All I know is we have to try.

Julius gets on the bus first. He looks directly at us. "Everything OK?" he asks, frowning.

I nod stiffly, my fingers entwining on my lap. He opens his mouth to ask us something but is interrupted by Nana pushing past him.

"Where you come from?" she demands.

I stiffly rest my elbow on the windowsill. "I've been here the whole time, Nana," I tell her.

She screws her eyes at me and I think we haven't got away with it, when she shakes her head and sits down.

Femi slides in beside me and she's breathing quickly, her hands shaking. I lay my hand on hers and squeeze it.

"Everything OK?" I ask, barely moving my mouth, my eyes fixed straight ahead. She gives a short nod.

"I told them you left through the fire escape. That you were playing a game."

The bus starts and the noise of the engine bellows around us.

"They bought that?"

She nods again. "Only because it's you, and you're always getting in trouble."

I sigh with relief as the bus shakes from side to side down the uneven road.

"Finally, being a disappointment has paid off," I say, my leg bouncing against the floor of the bus.

I bite down hard on my lip, trying to distract myself by looking out the window. Trying not to give anything away by looking behind me and checking if Brim is OK. Taking Brim seemed like such a good idea at the time, but now, on the bus, knowing he could be found any minute, I'm beginning to think this is the worst thing I could have done.

12

As we approach Brim's house, Smiley turns in front of me and mouths, *What now?*

I can hear my heart beating so fast, I'm afraid everyone else can hear it too.

As soon as Julius parks in the front yard, I tell them to go inside. I nudge Femi as she walks by.

"Tell me when the coast is clear."

She nods and gets off the bus. Julius leads Aunty Elsa and Nana into the house, talking about how hungry he is.

Brim sits up behind me. "The coast clear yet?" he asks.

I watch the front door, waiting for a sign. Minutes

later, Femi opens the door and beckons us inside. I take Brim's hand and rush him off the bus, across the gravelled front yard, and into the house.

"They're out back," Femi whispers, joining us. She walks ahead, while Smiley stands in the kitchen keeping an eye on the adults.

We reach our room and I lead Brim inside and sit him on the bed. Femi and Smiley follow, closing the door behind them.

The three of us stand in the middle of the room looking at Brim, who is looking around blankly.

"Now what?" Femi says.

I don't know what to do now that we have Brim here. We can't keep him hidden for ever.

"Ask him about the key," Smiley suggests.

Brim turns to look at her. "You know, this is the second time you talking like I'm not here," he grumbles.

Smiley looks sheepish. "Sorry."

I sit down next to Brim, knowing I don't have much time left.

"Brim," I say gently, "do you remember the secret door you built for Mama?"

He frowns. "Whose mama, your mama?"

I nod. "Yes! You said whoever found the secret door could keep what was behind it, and Mama found it."

He frowns, shaking his head. "I don't remember a door for Evelyn. I would remember that."

I sigh.

"Who's Evelyn?" Smiley whispers behind her hand.

I sink back onto the bed, deflated. "My grandma—his wife."

I frantically try to think of something that will trigger his memory. As we think about what to do with Brim, there is a bustle of voices in the hallway and one I recognize immediately.

My stomach does somersaults, and I clutch it, closing my eyes.

"What's going on out there?" Smiley says, confused, and before I can answer, there is a knock on the door.

I freeze, my heart suddenly jumping into my throat.

"Answer it," Femi hisses.

I take a deep breath and reluctantly edge over to the door. I grasp the handle, closing my eyes again and taking a deep breath.

I open the door a crack and peer out.

Aunty Elsa looks back at me, beaming. "Your father's here."

I shut the door immediately, pressing my back against it, a wave of nausea hitting me.

Aunty Elsa knocks again. "Brie? What happened? Did you hear me?"

I open my eyes and look at a horrified Femi and Smiley, and a confused Brim. I bite my fingernails worriedly, something I haven't done since I was nine. I try to think of what to do but my mind is swimming, and I can't think straight.

"Should we hide him?" Smiley hisses.

I take a deep breath and open the door again, just enough to slide through into the hall and close the door behind me.

Femi stays inside with Brim, and Smiley comes with me for moral support.

"You all right?" Aunty Elsa says, frowning. "You're shaking."

I nod stiffly but can't bring myself to speak. As we draw closer to the voices, my heart feels like it's going to explode out of my chest.

I step outside and the warm afternoon heat hits my skin like an oven.

"Look who I've found," Aunty Elsa announces.

Papa turns and his eyes brighten. He opens his arms. I shuffle over to him and allow him to hug me.

"Happy to see me?" he says, and I manage a "Mmm-hmm," into his chest. I pull away, afraid he might feel how fast my chest is rising and falling.

Smiley and I squeeze onto the one wooden chair nearest to the kitchen as they talk about Papa's work, how he put his foot down and demanded time off.

"I thought about all the fun you were having," he says. "I didn't want to miss out."

"That's nice, isn't it, Brie?" Aunty Elsa says, and now they are all looking at me.

I bite the inside of my lip, nodding stiffly. "Mmm-hmm," I repeat.

Nana clicks her teeth, shaking her head. "All she's wanted is to have you here and now she acting like she don't care."

I glance through the kitchen and down the hall to where my room is, trying to keep a sharp eye on it.

When I don't answer, Papa nudges me, making me jump. "You all right?" he says, bemused.

"She looks like she's seen a duppy," Nana says, and they all laugh, but I can't laugh with them. My mouth can barely move, and my throat is dry.

Aunty Elsa gets up to start lunch and I jump to my feet to help her, practically yanking the plates out of her hands.

My skin is sweating, my heart pounding. Smiley slides up to me, taking a plate out of my hand.

"Tell him," she hisses.

I glare at her, knowing Papa is watching and she could give it all away. She places the plate down on the wooden outside table and lowers her head.

"Brie, say something."

I take my time placing the plates around the table to give me enough time to think about how I'm going to tell Papa that I kidnapped Brim from the home. I think about Mama and how she would always take me off on adventures and how it would cause fights between her and Papa.

"You can't just run off with her and not tell me," he would say behind the closed door of their bedroom.

"We didn't plan it," Mama would reply. "It just happened. Stop fussing so much."

I remember the lines of worry on Papa's face when

he would ask Mama what her plans were that day and Mama would simply reply, "I don't know. My heart hasn't spoken to me yet."

I lay the last plate down and turn it left, then right. My heart is so loud Papa must be able to hear it. I don't know why I thought it was a good idea to kidnap Brim. What was I thinking? Papa is going to be so angry, and what about the home? They must have noticed Brim is gone by now.

As if on cue, the house phone rings. I freeze to the spot. Smiley grips my arm.

"How many times you going to turn that plate?" Nana calls over to me.

I take a deep breath and brace myself. This is it. Either I tell Papa now or it all comes out when someone answers that phone.

I turn slowly, my breathing so quick I think I might pass out.

"Brie!" Femi runs out and her eyes are wide like she's seen a ghost. "He's gone. Brim's gone."

I don't know what happened after that or in what order. It became a bit of a blur. Behind Femi, I can see Elsa picking up the phone and putting it to her ear. To the right, Papa jumps to his feet.

"What? Who's gone?" he shouts.

Next to him, Nana sits upright, looking confused, like she can't have heard right. Julius appears from somewhere asking what's going on because he missed it all and Nana tells him she doesn't know either.

Femi and Smiley are as frozen as I am, their hands covering their mouths, their eyes wide in disbelief.

Papa takes a step forward and tilts his head. "Who?" he repeats.

I suddenly find my feet and run into the kitchen just as Elsa says, "What do you mean he's not there?" into the phone.

I run by her, frantically mumbling, "Please no, please no," under my breath. I'm hoping, praying, that Femi got it wrong. I hear her behind me trying to whisper but now everyone is listening.

"I left for a few minutes to call Mama," she says. "I wasn't gone long, I swear."

I push the door open and allow it to hit the wall behind. I stand in the doorway and look over at the bed. Brim is not there.

I run to the bed and pull the sheets off. Maybe he went to sleep, and he's hidden under the covers, but the bed is empty.

"Bridgette." Papa's voice booms into the room and I dare not look at him. "Do you want to explain to me what is going on?"

He calls my name a few times as I run around the room opening cupboards and drawers because right now it doesn't matter where in the room he is, as long as he's here. Now telling Papa about taking him seems the least of my worries.

"Brie!" Nana's stern voice shouts over Papa's and I stop searching, gasping for breath as though I've run a mile.

"It's all my fault," I blurt out. "I brought Brim out of the home because he wasn't happy."

Papa and Nana glare at me and Papa's face is like thunder.

"You did what?"

I can't breathe. I slump against the wall, my hands against my knees as I try to catch my breath.

Papa puts his anger and disappointment to one side to organize a search for Brim. We search the house. Every room, every cupboard, under the sofa, behind the curtain. We move outside and search the yard, calling his name, but no Brim.

Papa spreads us out. He sends Smiley and Femi

back in the house to check again. He asks Aunty Elsa to come with him to check the road. Julius suggests driving the bus to look for him. Nana says she will check the bottom of the garden.

"I'll check the beach and the caves," I suggest, but Papa gives me a stern look.

"I'll check the caves," Julius says. "We can go together."

Papa leaves us without saying a word, and Elsa follows him around the house to the front and they disappear out of sight.

Nana walks with us down to the end of the garden, shouting Brim's name. I follow at a distance, feeling sick to my stomach.

If we lose Brim, it will be all my fault and I will never forgive myself.

"He can't have gone far." Julius slows down to allow me to catch up with him. "When we find him, we have to face your father," he says as we walk out onto the beach. He stops and sighs loudly, but his voice is lost under the waves. "And neither of us wants that."

I know he's trying to make me smile, but all it does is make it worse. I've disappointed Papa a lot lately, but this must be the worst thing I have ever done.

"Look," Julius says, pointing to the end of the beach. There, sitting on a large rock, the only rock in the sand, is a small, dark figure. I run over to him as fast as my legs will carry me and throw myself on Brim, almost toppling him over.

"Watch it," he says in his usual gentle voice.

I bend down in front of him, my legs getting lost in the sand. "Papa Brim," I say, on the verge of tears, "we've been looking everywhere for you."

Julius reaches us and pats Brim on the shoulder. "You gave us a scare there, Brim," he says, and there is relief in his voice.

Brim nods, looking out to sea. "I don't want to be cooped up any more," he says. "I want to be free. You can help me stay free, Dee?"

I catch Julius's surprised look. It's the first time he's heard Brim call me by Mama's name.

"You can help me?" he asks again. This time he is looking directly at me.

I sit back on my legs and bite my bottom lip, not knowing what to say.

I look around me suddenly, as a thought hits me. "Brim, how did you get here without us seeing you?"

His hand moves to his neck, and he pulls out a necklace to show me. "With the key, of course," he says. "I always use the key."

13

Papa sends me to my room. All of us. Me, Femi and Smiley. We sit on the edge of the bed in silence, listening to Julius and Papa arguing outside in the backyard.

"How did you not see them take an old man?" Papa is saying.

Smiley jumps to her feet and cracks the door open. She peers down the hall. "He's mad," she says. "He's walking up and down really angry."

"Oh." She squints through the crack. "Oh no."

I jump to my feet and run over to the door. We peer through the crack and down the hall. To the front of the house, in the living room, Aunty Elsa is sitting with Brim on the tree-shaped chair and the sound of the TV is blocking out what is going on outside.

Nana stands by the door of the kitchen, occasionally attempting to calm Julius and Papa down but neither of them is listening to her.

"Stop acting like one of the children!" Papa shouts. "You a grown man. You should have stopped them. You should have told me, her father."

Julius shakes his head. "She wanted to take her grandfather home, because he was barely alive in there. She wanted him here, and he wants to be here. What's so wrong with that?"

Julius starts heading back into the house, then stops and half turns. "You know, if you just listened to her, you would see she is just like her mother. Dee would have done the same thing. She would have got him out of there."

Julius storms through the house with a face like thunder and I don't think I have ever seen him this mad. I don't think I have ever seen him mad at all. We all crane our necks to watch as he storms through the living room.

"Where are you going?" Aunty Elsa cries, but

Julius only yanks the front door open and marches out. She jumps to her feet and follows him outside.

We turn our heads back down the hall and Papa is glaring after him with his arms folded across his chest. His eyes catch us peering through the crack of the door.

"Close it, close it," Smiley hisses, and we slam the door shut.

*

Long after the girls have fallen asleep around me, I lie wide awake, thinking of how badly I have messed things up. Things were bad enough between me and Papa. Ever since Mama died, we have grown further and further apart. Everything I do seems to annoy him, and now I have made things worse. I twist my fingers under the sheet. There doesn't seem any way out of this. I've really messed up this time.

At some point in the night, I hear Papa telling Brim to put his shoes on.

"I don't want to!" Brim shouts, and he sounds so upset that I jump out of bed and open the door.

Down the hall, Brim is sitting in the living room and Papa is on his knees tying his laces. I tiptoe out of my room and down the hall, stopping at the doorway in the shadows.

"Papa, please let him stay," I beg him.

But Papa doesn't answer. Instead, he gets to his feet and gently helps Brim to his. He fidgets around for something and finds the keys to the bus on the small table by the door. Julius must have left the bus.

He opens the front door for Brim who is still moaning, and I follow, barefooted.

"Papa, please, he hates it there," I beg, just loud enough for him to hear but not enough to wake the house.

"Go to bed, Brie," he says sternly without looking at me.

Brim becomes even more hysterical, screaming Mama's name. He gets so loud that Papa relents and lets me get on the bus.

"Before we wake the neighbourhood. Hurry," he says wearily, so I run barefoot out onto the gravelled front yard in my grey pyjama shorts and T-shirt and onto the bus. I sit next to Brim at the front of the bus and take his trembling hand into my own.

"It's OK, Brim," I reassure him, but I don't believe it any more than he does.

Papa sits behind the wheel and starts the engine, and I can't help but remember the last time we were on this bus, so excited to see Brim, still thinking about Mama's letter and the secret door. Things have changed so much since then. Now the letters are like a distant memory and Papa will probably take me home tomorrow. My eyes become watery with tears of frustration that it's ending this way. That Papa Brim is being forced to go back and that Papa doesn't understand why I took him out, but more than that, I wish he had stayed home. Things were so much better without him.

*

It takes some time for Papa to turn the long bus around in the front yard. It's pitch-black outside with only one streetlamp to guide him. The longer it takes him to get out, the more frustrated he gets, and the more frustrated he gets, the angrier I get.

When we finally get onto the road, we drive in heavy silence. Not even Brim speaks as the old bus rumbles down the narrow road. It's hard to see outside. I have visions of a truck, or another bus, coming around the corner and Papa having nowhere to go. I am relieved when we reach the bright lights of Bridgetown. I'm surprised to see it's still busy even though the shops have closed. People hang out on the side of the road, while music blasts from an open car boot with a large speaker inside. A man serves food from a drum like Jackfruit, and next to him a woman sells drinks and snacks on a rickety wooden table. Papa drives through the town without stopping and eventually the roads become quiet again. This time there are plenty of streetlamps lighting our way and the drive is smoother.

Not long after, he turns down the familiar path and through the open gates. The bus shakes as he manoeuvres the stones and ditches underneath. He stops the bus outside the same house and beeps his horn. The same woman comes out, and she is dressed casually this time, in a pair of grey shorts and a striped vest. I grip Brim's hand tightly. Papa switches on the light in the bus and turns.

"Papa, please," I beg him again.

"Don't say another word," he says, and his voice is deep and filled with so much rage that I drop Brim's hand. Papa leads Brim off the bus and he and the lady walk him up the path and disappear into the night.

I sit alone on the bus, my heart pounding against my chest. Upset that Brim had to go back, mad at Papa for taking him. It's there I stay, chest rising and falling fast, until Papa appears out of the darkness, alone. He climbs into the bus and gets back into the driver's seat, closing the door.

He hangs his head and I think maybe he's fallen asleep, but then he sits upright, sighs loudly, starts the engine and turns the bus in the small space.

We drive back in silence, along the brightly lit road that is almost empty, through the busy town and towards Brim's Island again.

"He can't stay with us, Brie," he says suddenly, glancing at me in the mirror. "He needs looking after, and who would do that? Elsa? She works. Me? I work. Nana? You?"

I know what he's doing. Trying to prove a point. Trying to say he's right and I'm wrong. I stare hard out the window, purposely ignoring him. If he really cared about Brim, he would find a way. But all he cares about is work and money. All he cares about is himself.

We pull up to Brim's house and Papa turns off the engine. He sighs and all I can see is the back of his head and the crease of skin in the back of his neck. He turns in his seat and looks at me, though his face is in shadow. I can't tell if he's still mad; I can't see his expression.

"I know you think your mama would have wanted you to do that," he says, and his voice sounds tired, "but, Brie, your mother did a lot of things that seemed fun but weren't right."

I feel my chest tighten.

"She was fun and adventurous, but what you didn't see was the aftermath. The mess I had to clean up, the people I had to call to say sorry, she meant no harm." He pauses, lowering his head, his shoulders hunched. "It's only fun if people don't get hurt, and that's the line she couldn't walk. It's what she taught you, it's why you think it's OK, but it's not. It's not OK."

I sit rooted to the spot as he climbs out of the front seat and opens the doors of the bus. He turns and waits for me. I want to tell him to leave me alone. That I will never forgive him for talking about Mama that way, for taking Brim back, for always letting me down.

I clench my fists and feel something. I look down at my hand. I take a sharp intake of breath. A silver necklace lies crumpled in the palm of my hand—and attached to it is a key.

*

Papa watches me enter my bedroom and close the door behind me. I listen with my ear against the door and wait for him to settle on Brim's wooden sofa for the night. Smiley and Femi are fast asleep, so I slide to the floor, leaning against the door to bide some time until he falls asleep.

I sit crouched on the floor in the dark, staring at the key Brim gave me. The straight silver edge with a round head and zigzag lines. I don't remember seeing him take off the necklace or feeling anything when he placed it in my hand. Now I don't know if he did it because he remembered who I was or if he still thought I was Mama and wanted me to have it.

A movement in the dark startles me. Femi slides out of bed and tiptoes across the room to the chest of drawers. She scrolls through her phone, then lays it back down and turns, jumping out of her skin.

"What are you doing?" she cries, spotting me on the floor.

"What are you doing?" I ask suspiciously.

She tiptoes over to me and sits on the floor beside me. "Just checking my phone." She sighs.

I give her the side eye. "For who? It's late."

"My mum. I haven't heard from her since I got here," she says, shrugging the answer away.

"Is she OK?"

She nods, staring at her fingers. "I asked your dad and he said he saw her. He asked her if she wanted to come with him, but she was too busy."

I feel a pang of sympathy for her. Femi's parents don't spend much time with her unless it has to do with school. She spends most of her time alone in the house because her parents work long hours.

"At least she's not on your case all the time like my papa," I tell her.

She falls silent. "I would rather have that," she says quietly, and I'm taken by surprise.

"Swap?" I joke. I offer her my hand. She takes it and shakes it.

"So, what are you doing?" she asks, changing the subject.

I show her the key, and her eyes light up. "You got it?"

I nod. "Brim gave it to me." I shake my head as she frowns. "It's a long story. I'll tell you another time. I'm waiting for Papa to fall asleep so I can look for the secret door."

"Can't it wait until the morning?" she asks, yawning.

I shake my head, knowing I may not have enough time in the morning. Papa might take me back home. "No, it's got to be tonight," I tell her firmly.

She nods. "OK," she says, and leans back against the door to wait.

*

I wake to Femi shaking me. "I think he's asleep," she whispers.

I rub my eyes and adjust to the dark. The sound of a train echoes from outside the room. It takes me some time to realize that it isn't a train, but Papa snoring. We get to our feet, and I slowly open the door and peer out. We tiptoe out of the room and into the hall.

Where do we start? Femi mouths.

I point towards the kitchen, and she follows me as we tiptoe past Nana's room and Aunty Elsa's.

In the kitchen, we spread out to look for the hidden door with a keyhole. We open every cupboard and press everything that sticks out of the wall or the floor, but nothing happens. We tiptoe down the hall, pressing every inch of the wall in case it's a fake wall that might turn out to be a door. We arrive in the living room, where Papa is sleeping.

I point Femi to one side of the room, and I take the other. We try everything that moves without waking Papa, but nothing has a keyhole and nothing opens.

There is only one place we haven't checked. Femi and I stand in front of the sofa Papa is sleeping on. He sleeps on his back, his mouth open, his arms crossed in front of him the way he does when he's about to tell me off for something. Even in his sleep he can't relax.

Femi and I exchange looks, then nod. We creep towards the sofa and timidly feel around the bottom, then the sides, nothing. We stand, frowning.

Femi nudges me and points to Papa. "What if it's under him?" she whispers.

We both turn to look at him, only to be met with Papa's open eyes looking back at us. We jump backward, holding in our screams. I wait for him to ask what we are doing, but then he closes his eyes again and turns onto his side.

It is enough for us, and we both run back to our room, shutting the door behind us before dissolving into uncontrollable laughter.

"What's going on?" a bleary-eyed Smiley says as we finally get into bed. She doesn't wait for an answer and falls back asleep. I lie in bed wide awake, touching the key around my neck.

Something about it feels special, like I am part of something. Something only Mama and I share. Something Papa can't take away from me as long as I don't tell him. This will be our secret, mine and Mama's, just like the old days. Just like before.

*

I wake suddenly. I don't know why. It's still dark in the room. The curtains are closed, and Femi and Smiley are still asleep beside me. I rummage around on the windowsill to check my phone. It's three a.m.

Smiley is curled around me. I can barely move, but I have this sudden urge to get up.

I peel Smiley off me and slide across their bodies until my feet touch the floor.

I feel the key around my neck. I want to find this door. Something is pulling me, and I can't seem to rest until I respond. I walk slowly around the room, racking my brain about where this door could be. It wasn't in the kitchen or in the living room. The only places we haven't checked are Aunty Elsa's and Nana's rooms, and I can't get in while they're sleeping. Nana is a light sleeper. I've tried sneaking into her room before to sleep next to her. Not long after Mama died, I was scared to sleep alone. I kept thinking Mama would return as a ghost and haunt me, and the thought scared me so much, I couldn't fall asleep.

I get down on my knees and reach for her box of letters from underneath the bed. Maybe I missed a clue. Maybe if I read the letters again, they will tell me where the door is. I slide the box out and open it gingerly, trying not to wake the others.

I read through the letters again. The first letter where she tells me about the letters, the second where she tells me about the secret, and the third where she gives me a clue. I read the letters over and over, but there is nothing. I sigh, disappointed that I will have to wait until the morning to continue looking. I slide the box back under the bed, as far back as it will go so no one will find it, and as I do, something catches my eye that I didn't see before, something gold. I lie flat on my stomach and stretch my hand to touch it. My heart starts to pound inside my chest. I jump to my feet and climb over the girls to grab my phone. Lying flat on my stomach, I shine the torch on my phone under the bed and a loud gasp escapes me.

A keyhole.

14

My hands are shaking as I unhook the key from the necklace. I hold it in my hand and reach under the bed, trying to match the key to the lock. It's harder than I thought. With only a side view of the keyhole, located under a bed with two people sleeping on it, I keep missing the hole. I can feel myself getting angry at the stupid lock, and at myself for not being able to do something so simple. For being so close to the end but not able to go any further.

I take a deep breath and try again. Slowly this time, carefully, as though I am defusing a bomb. I line the key above the hole and slowly, carefully bring it down.

It fits.

"Yes!" I cry with relief, then freeze to see if I have woken anyone.

No one moves, so I turn the key and there is a click. Nothing moves. No door opens. I press the tiles under the bed. Nothing. I press the tiles around the lock, still nothing. I push and then pull. There is another click, and suddenly the tiles under the bed start to move outward, revealing stairs going down.

I stare down into the dark hole in disbelief, my chest pounding with nervousness and excitement. I slide on my stomach into the hole and find the first step of a ladder; then with the light from my phone guiding me, I go down as far as it will take me.

The ladder ends and I step onto a rocky floor. I move the light of my phone around. I am in a small cave. One of the many caves that are under this house. There is nothing here but rocks sticking out of the walls. I don't know what I expected, but it wasn't this.

My shoulders slump as I look around the empty cave. Is this it? Is this what Mama wanted me to see? I spin around, shining the torch around me and above me, looking for something else. This can't be it. The door to the cave was hidden, so maybe... I walk over to the walls of the cave and touch the stone. It is cold and damp. I press. Nothing. I move around the cave, pressing and pushing stones, hoping, praying that something will move. Then, directly across from the ladder, a section of rock looks different from the others. I stare at it, run my finger around it. It feels... fake? I press it and there is a click before the stone opens, revealing another lock.

I feel around in my pocket for the key and realize I have left it in the lock upstairs. I rush up the ladder, grab the key from the lock, and rush back down, almost missing a step.

I push the key into the lock. It fits. I can barely breathe. I push and the entire rock face moves. I push again and it opens like a door, revealing nothing I have ever seen before.

In front of me there is an open cove filled with greenery, towering trees and jutting rocks. I step onto the soft grassy ground beneath me. A bird chirps overhead and lands on a tree that is as tall as the highest rock. The moonlight twinkles in between the trees, and pink and yellow flowers grow wildly around the tree trunk. I climb over a large rock and down the other side onto a tiny, gravelled path that winds through the trees. It is quiet but it feels alive. Like animals live here that have never been seen before, like this is their world. A world filled with sunshine and trees and water trickling from a hole in the rock.

There are too many things to see as I follow the path around the rock face. Ahead, there is an archway carved into the rock as tall as the sky. Through the archway is a tiny circular cove. The ground is covered in green grass and the sky acts as a roof to the cave.

There is nothing in here but a bench against the rock on my left, so I approach it, still in disbelief that I have found Mama's secret place. Carved into the wooden seat are the words

DEE 1987

She was twelve. The same age I am now. My fingers tremble as I run my hand over each letter, as though I can feel her with every curve in the wood. I kneel on the ground, not caring that I'm in my pyjamas, and I stare at her name in wonder, and pain, and sadness.

The tears roll down my cheeks like rain. Everything I have been holding on to, all the pain I have been hiding, comes rushing out.

Through the tears, my eyes catch a glint of something behind the bench. A gap in the rock face and something inside. I reach inside and feel around until my fingers grasp it and pull it out. It's a tin. I sit on the bench and pry it open. Inside is an envelope. The same envelope as all the others. This time it simply says:

BRIE

I pull the letter out of the envelope and unfold it.

My Dearest Brie,

If you read this, it is because you have cracked the code. You have solved the clues and now you are in my secret place.

When Brim built this house, he wanted it to be a place of wonder and adventure, but more than that, he wanted me to never stop exploring, never stop being inquisitive.

He bought this land because of these caves. He already knew what he wanted to do with it. I knew he wanted to give me a fairy tale land I would never tire of. Something to keep my mind occupied. Somewhere I could escape when I needed peace. Somewhere I could go that was mine.

I have spent many hours here, crying over friends I've lost and boys who lost me. Screaming into the void over rules I wanted to break. I have spent hours here thinking, laughing, dancing, creating, and learning who I was and who I wanted to be without distraction.

To have something that was mine was the best gift Brim could have ever given me. No one ever came here but me. No one was allowed to. It was my space, and looking back, I realize how important that was.

It was when I told your father this story and shared with him for the first time about my secret cave and how much I wished you could have seen it, that he suggested writing these letters to you, so we could be together in spirit just like the old times.

Your father was the one who sat with me and planned our final adventure. It was he who helped me with the clues, he who promised to hold on to it until you were the right age. It was he who agreed that this was what you needed.

So, Brie, my darling. I hand this over to you. At the same age I received it. This is yours and yours only. I hope you find peace here when you are sad. I hope you find laughter when you are happy. I hope you come here to find the answers you need. More than that, I hope that you will find me.

Love Always,
Your Mama

I sit for some time reading the letter over and over until the tears dry. So, Papa knew about it all along.

He wasn't just holding the letters for her; it was his idea to write them.

I sink back on my legs and stare off into the distance as I go over everything that has happened. I grimace at the way I treated him. The things I said in my head, the things I said out loud. All the time I thought Papa didn't care about the letters or me, when the letters were his idea all along.

*

"Brie, come out of your room. We have visitors," Nana calls, peering into my room.

I don't know how long I have been sleeping but the sun is shining bright into the room and the bed is empty.

She frowns at me. "Why you so tired?"

I feel the necklace against my chest and run my finger along the key. A smile pulls at my lips as I remember what is under the bed.

I climb out of bed and throw some clothes on, emerging in the hallway, where I hear chatter coming from outside.

There is a small breeze wafting into the house

from the sea. The trees sway gently from side to side and a bird flies overhead.

Last night seems like a dream. I keep touching the key to remind myself that it happened. I want to go back there. I feel so close to Mama down in the caves but I haven't decided if I will show it to anyone yet, or even tell them about it. I like having something that is only mine and Mama's and now Papa's too. He's the only other person apart from Brim who knows.

As I enter the kitchen, I see Paulton outside. Smiley runs in when she spots me. She grabs my hand with a little squeal that only I can hear.

"Where have you been?" she whispers. "We've been waiting for you, and it's been so awkward. He asked me something and I didn't hear what he said, so I laughed, and now he's looking at me weird."

I look behind her where Paulton is standing against the veranda post. He's dressed in jeans, a white T-shirt and a matching jean jacket. His short dreads swing as he looks from one adult to the other.

"He's not looking," I reassure her.

She sighs in relief and follows me outside.

Paulton's mother is talking to Julius, and I am surprised to see her, but I am more surprised to see Julius after last night. Paulton's mother jumps up from the outdoor chairs and she holds her arms out to me.

"Brie," she says, holding me at arm's length. "Look at you, how you've grown. Hasn't she grown, Paulton?" She glances over at Paulton, who shrugs. For some reason this makes the adults laugh.

"Oh, he's gone all shy," Nana says, pinching his cheek.

"Do you remember when they used to call each other brother and sister?" Paulton's mother says, beaming.

"They were five," Papa says quietly. He doesn't say good morning to me or ask about last night, but he and Julius seem to have made up and I can't help but wonder what was said.

Papa's eyes fall to my hand around the key. He catches my eye and smiles. I smile back, a knowing smile, a smile only we understand. A secret only we share.

"Paulton has a football match this afternoon down at the Mango Hall playing field," Paulton's mother says, standing tall in white pants that reach her ankles and an orange blouse tucked in. "Paulton wants you all to come along if you're free."

Paulton shifts from one foot to the other. "We both want you to come," he says, staring at the tiled veranda.

She runs her hand over his hair. "Yes, we both want you to come," she says, winking.

"Well, who you playing?" Julius asks, sitting sideways in his seat. "I only go see the best teams."

Paulton's mother nudges him.

"We playing the next town," Paulton says.

"They any good?" Papa asks.

Paulton grins. "Not as good as us, but they all right."

This sends the adults into fits of laughter and Julius high-fives him. Adults are weird. They find the weirdest things funny.

Smiley nudges me. "Maybe we can pretend to be sick and stay behind to look for the door." She coughs loudly.

I run my finger along the key, remembering the cave below us.

"No, let's go to the game," I tell her. "Besides, you want to see him play football, don't you?"

I wrap my arm around her as she tries to hide her smile.

"I guess we should support your friend," she says, holding a smile in.

I nod with a serious face. "It's the right thing to do."

We collapse in peals of laughter.

*

Mango Hall is on the outskirts of Bridgetown on a strip of road that is full of fields and the odd building. The field sits between a small brick building used for indoor sports and a primary school on the other side. The road is crowded with parked cars and vendors selling takeaway food and snacks. Cars line each side of the road, and someone is playing a loud sound system. It's not easy to park a large bus, but Papa manages to manoeuvre it between a white Toyota and a minibus with help from a man passing by shouting instructions from behind.

When we get off the bus, there are swarms of people heading towards the field wearing their favourite team colours. We join the crowd and head onto the field, which is already packed with people.

Rows of benches are placed around the perimeter, every one of them full.

Paulton runs off to join his team while we try to find somewhere to sit. Aunty Elsa eventually finds a patch of grass and she lays out blankets she brought from the house for us to sit on. Julius sets up a few folding chairs he brought for the adults.

Someone starts playing a drum over the sound system, while certain parts of the crowd shout their team chants. I sit down on the blanket at the edge of the field next to Femi and Smiley.

Aunty Elsa opens a bag filled with food and starts laying out sandwiches and drinks on the blankets. A horn blows and the two teams run onto the field. The crowd erupts into cheers.

"Go, Paulton!" Julius screams at the top of his voice.

Nana glares at him. "Right in mi ear," she complains, turning away.

Julius grabs her face and gives her a kiss. I spot Papa standing away from us and my hand moves to the key around my neck. I can't stop thinking about the letter Mama wrote in the cave. When she said the letters were Papa's idea. I'm about to get to my feet and go over to him when he approaches us.

"I have some business to do," he says.

My shoulders fall and I sit back down.

"Right now?" Nana asks, nodding towards me.

Papa nods. "Yes, right now, but I'll see you back at the house."

I feel him kiss me on top of my head, but by the time I turn, he is already walking away. After that the game becomes a blur. I want to tell Papa I know he told Mama to write the letters. I thought it might be the beginning of something new for us, but it's hard to try with Papa when he never sticks around.

15

Paulton's team wins 3–2, and after the match we head back home on the bus. Nana decides she wants to try driving the bus even when Julius tells her it isn't a good idea.

"Why, because I'm a woman?" Nana snaps, getting behind the wheel.

Julius raises his hand and sits down. Nana takes off, driving like the bus has no brakes or she doesn't know where they are. She cuts corners and drives on the kerb. One woman screams at us as she tries to cross the road, but Nana doesn't seem to notice.

Paulton's mother spends the entire journey squealing every time Nana turns a corner.

"You going to kill us!" she says with her hand pressed against her heart. She is relieved when we reach home and is the first to get off the bus. She kneels on the ground and kisses it.

Nana invites them in for the evening. Paulton whispers something to his mother and she accepts. We enter the house, chattering non-stop about our day. About how Paulton is a champion footballer. Between it all, Smiley is still pleading with me to look for the secret door.

The back door is open and soft music is coming from outside. The tables are already laid and the familiar fairy lights are turned on.

We all stop talking abruptly, wondering who could have done all this. We step outside and Papa is in the garden trimming the plants with Brim; Julius is with the others.

I stop short, my mouth falling open. "Brim?"

He glances up at me. "Dee, where you been?"

I look to Nana in shock.

"Nothing to do with me," she says, nodding towards Papa.

I look at Papa, puzzled. "Is that where you went today, to pick up Brim?"

He nods with a smile. "Julius and I had a long talk and we came up with an arrangement." He nods to Julius, who is beaming. "Every weekend, Brim comes home. What do you think about that?"

"Home with us?" I ask, hopeful.

Papa weighs it up. "Well, we were thinking we would split the weekends. One with us and one here."

My insides feel like they are floating I am so happy; I run over to him and throw myself on him.

"Thank you, Papa," I whisper. That means I get to see Brim every week and I get to visit Mama's secret cave. My heart is dancing, and I can't stop smiling. It's as if everything is coming together. Just when I thought they were falling apart again.

Julius challenges everyone to a game of dominoes while dinner cooks and Brim stops what he's doing.

"Nobody can play dominoes like me," he says, rushing onto the patio.

Paulton pats him on the back. "I'm on your team, then, Brim," he says.

I walk out into the garden where Papa is clearing up. I think about Mama's secret place, and her letters. I think about how he has kept this a secret for so long without ever giving me a clue that he knew.

"I'm mad at Mama," I tell him with my heart in my mouth, "and I'm mad at you."

I don't mean for it to come out this way, but it does and now that it's out, my heart is pounding. For a moment Papa says nothing and I'm too scared to look to see if he's mad, or if he's getting ready to tell me what a terrible person I am.

He stands and I feel his hand on me. He sighs, and all I can hear is Smiley's voice on the veranda screaming, "Cheat! They cheated!"

"Come," he says quietly, "let's talk."

We walk down to the bottom of the garden, and he stops.

"Do you remember that summer when it rained almost every day?" he asks out of the blue.

I do remember. It was one of the few times he spent the entire summer here with us.

"Your mother had made a picnic and we sat under the sweetsop tree, and it was the only dry day, so the tree was a nice shade. Maybe we should go there, just you and me?"

I nod and we head to the sweetsop tree where the moon shines bright like a night lamp and guides us. Brim had made a wooden seat under the tree, and in the dark, we can just make out the words Dee carved into the back of the seat.

We sit down and Papa turns to me, concerned. "Tell me what you're mad at." He leans away from me, covering his head. "I'm ready."

I laugh the kind of laugh that's mixed with nerves. I don't see Papa being silly, not any more.

"Is it OK to be mad at her?" I mumble.

"Why you mad?" he asks.

"I'm mad because she wore big hats and big clothes and heels when the road was uneven," I tell him.

Papa laughs loudly, throwing his head back. "She didn't care, did she?" he says.

His laughter prompts me on. "I'm mad that she always wanted me to take a picture of her and take videos, and dance. I hate dancing."

He leans back onto the tree, his body shaking with laughter. It feels good to see him laughing. It feels even better that it is because of me.

"And that time I was forced to do the school play and I didn't want to and she came to the front of the stage while I was doing my solo and sang all the words really loud."

His laughter dies down and he wipes the tears from his eyes. "Your mama was unique," he says, nodding in agreement. "Not perfect, but she was ours. She loved us like no one else could." He stares at his hands. "She loved intensely. She was loud, and stubborn and wild." His voice breaks and he looks over at me. "And we loved you to the moon and back. I'm sorry for not telling you that enough."

He pats my leg, then suddenly pulls me into his chest, and I can hear his heart beating fast.

"I'm not perfect either," he whispers into my hair, "but I'm learning how to be mum and dad. I'm learning how to earn money and be there for you. I'm learning to be better. But you can help me. We can help each other."

It's strange hearing Papa talk like this. I wish I had heard this sooner; maybe I wouldn't have been so mad at him for so long. Maybe I would have understood why he needs to work, maybe we could have talked about it.

I rest my head on his chest and it feels like home.

"Thank you for the letters, Papa," I whisper. "It's the best present ever, and I'll never forget it."

He kisses my forehead and wraps his arms around me.

*

That evening, we eat another meal outside that Julius cooked for everyone. He can't stop telling us he cooked it all by himself. Aunty Elsa has to tell him to shush and sit down. Papa seems happier and more relaxed than usual. He gets into a debate with Femi about music. It's a cool evening, perfect for being outside. Everything seems just the way I want it, with all my family and my two best friends.

Smiley leans over to me and whispers, "Paulton went home?" She pulls a sad face.

I laugh, shaking my head. "Well, I'll invite him to come and see us the weekend of the school dance, if you ask him to go with you."

Her eyes widen and her mouth falls open. "I can't do that!" she exclaims.

I think about Mama's letters and how they all come back to one thing, living. I take a bite of boiled dumpling. "You can do anything you want, Smiley. I believe in you."

She throws her arms around me. "OK," she says, hyping herself up. "I'll do it."

As the evening sets and dinner ends, I take Nana to one side and whisper something to her. Her face lights up and she leads me inside. Ten minutes later, we return with a bunch of clothes in our hands.

Everyone is still chattering around the table and Nana calls for their attention.

"Listen up," she says. "Brie has something to say." She turns to me and nods with a smile.

"These are some of Mama's things," I say, looking down at the feather boa around my neck, the jacket and long flowy skirt in my hand. "She was always leaving things here."

"And everywhere," Nana jokes.

I nod, smiling. Mama did do that.

"I thought that maybe tonight, we can each wear something of hers?" I look up, feeling silly. Now that the letters have ended and I have found her secret cave, now that Papa and I are getting along better, it seems only right to do something Mama would have loved.

It's what she would have wanted.

Papa is the first to his feet. "I'll take the hat." He snatches Mama's signature oversized straw hat from me and places it on his head, but his head is too big, and it makes everyone laugh. He doesn't frown and look all serious like he normally does. Instead, he strikes a pose that is kind of embarrassing before I remember the things Mama used to do that would embarrass me and how I miss them now. I would endure her embarrassing dances every day if I could and I would not complain. Not once.

Nana takes another sunhat, claiming it's actually hers, not Mama's. Femi takes a blue jacket that Mama always wore over her dresses in the evenings when the wind was cool. Smiley takes one of Mama's many feather boas from her birthday parties.

Julius takes her red wig, and Papa and Aunty Elsa take another feather boa. I give Brim her sunglasses. I slip on her long skirt over my jeans and wrap her purple feather boa around me.

We dance down the garden like Mama would, floating, arms waving around. We make our way down to the beach, where Julius lights a bonfire, and Smiley challenges Papa to a game of football in the sand. I see Brim sitting on a rock by the bonfire, staring off in the distance. I go over and sit down beside him.

"You OK, Brim?" I ask, leaning my head on his shoulder. At first, he doesn't answer, and I think he may not have heard me. "Brim?"

Finally, as if coming out of his trance, he says quietly, "Sometimes I feel like I'm waking up from a dream, Brie."

My heart skips a beat. He said my name. Not Mama's, mine, so maybe he's not going to forget any more. Maybe his memory is coming back and so is the old Brim. He nods again as if answering the same question.

"But we will be all right," he says, patting the key around my neck. "Don't you worry about a thing."

I slip my hand into his and rest my head on his shoulder as the moon glimmers across the water.

*

Dear Mama,

Thanks for the letters. I wish you were here. I had a big birthday. Everyone came. There was lots of food and presents and music. Yes, I am still friends with Smiley—she is my best friend—and I'm now friends with a girl called Femi too. She moved here two years ago.

Lots of things happened because of your letters.

We came to Brim's Island without Papa, and I kidnapped Brim out of the home. You couldn't have known that Brim was going to be in a home when you wrote your letters. Papa didn't like me bringing Brim home, so he got mad and took him back.

Remember Paulton? He's some super-star football player now. He took us to one of his games and he won.

Your letters finally brought us all together. Papa left work, and he brought Brim back to stay with us. Now we're going to see him every weekend.

I thought Papa would never care about me the way you did, but now I realize he always cared, just in a different way.

When I think about it, I think maybe that's what you wanted the letters to do. To bring us together because that's what you were always good at.

But the best thing I got out of the letters was the secret door. Your special place. I found it, and it's the best place I have ever seen. Thank you, Mama.

When I go there, it's going to be like you never left. Like a piece of you is still here, so now it's my happy place and I will cherish it for ever.

I Love You Always,

Brie x

While everyone is distracted outside, I slip into the room and lock the door behind me. I take the key from around my neck and unlock the door under the bed. I climb down the rusty ladder and into the first cave. I walk over to the rock and press it, slip the key in and turn it.

When the door opens, I step into the forest, climb over the rocks, and follow the path into the round cave with the bench with Mama's name on it. I take the letter I have written to her out of my pocket, and I slip it into the gap in the wall where I found my last letter; then I leave.

*

"Everyone in?" Papa shouts as we all climb onto the bus and find our seats.

We had said goodbye to Brim that morning, but it was OK knowing I would see him in a week.

Paulton waves from the side of the road while we tease Smiley.

Papa closes the door of the bus and starts the engine. "Everybody have a good time?" he shouts, pulling the bus away from the house and down the road.

"Yesss!" we all shout.

"Bye, Brim's Island," Smiley shouts, waving out the window.

"I'll miss you," Femi says, copying Smiley.

I peer out, my face pressed against the glass.

I feel for the key around my neck and wrap it in my hands.

Goodbye, Brim's Island. Goodbye, Mama's cave. See you soon.

We created Pushkin Children's Books to share tales from different languages and cultures with younger readers, and to open the door to the wide, colourful worlds these stories offer.

From picture books and adventure stories to fairy tales and classics, and from fifty-year-old bestsellers to current huge successes abroad, the books on the Pushkin Children's list reflect the very best stories from around the world, for our most discerning readers of all: children.

THE MURDERER'S APE
SALLY JONES AND THE FALSE ROSE
THE LEGEND OF SALLY JONES

Jakob Wegelius

WHEN LIFE GIVES YOU MANGOES
IF YOU READ THIS

Kereen Getten

BOY 87
LOST
MELT
FAKE

Ele Fountain

THE LETTER FOR THE KING
THE SECRETS OF THE WILD WOOD
THE SONG OF SEVEN
THE GOLDSMITH AND THE MASTER THIEF

Tonke Dragt

HOW TO BE BRAVE
HOW TO BE TRUE

Daisy May Johnson

THE MYSTERY OF THE MISSING MUM

Frances Moloney

LAMPIE

Annet Schaap

THE MISSING BARBEGAZZI
THE HUNGRY GHOST

H.S. Norup

SCHOOL FOR NOBODIES
THE THREE IMPOSSIBLES
THE DANGEROUS LIFE OF OPHELIA BOTTOM

Susie Bower

THE ELEPHANT
MY BROTHER BEN

Peter Carnavas

LENNY'S BOOK OF EVERYTHING
DRAGON SKIN

Karen Foxlee